HAPPY DANCE'N COWBOY

Billionaire Cowboys of Lone Star, Texas,
Book Four

HOPE
MOORE

Happy Dance'n Cowboy

Copyright © 2022 Hope Moore

This book is a work of fiction. Names and characters are of the author's imagination or are used fictitiously. Any resemblance to an actual person, living or dead, is entirely coincidental.

Happy Dance'n Cowboy

He's a happy-go-lucky cowboy who enjoys dancing, appreciates life, and loves being single… She's a woman with a hard past and now working even harder to make the right moves…and life is looking up—but it's a no go for romance…trust is something she no longer has.

Caleb Buckley enjoys watching his brothers and cousins fall in love, and he's really enjoying the town's newfound love of holding a dance once a month for all those who want to come into town to have a good time. He has no plans to settle down, but lately his attention is snagged by the quiet beauty who is working at the ladies' clothing store. The one who doesn't dance with anyone. The one whose stance and beautiful eyes clearly say "keep away".

Jasmine Scott has a past she's determined to leave behind. And after her mother introduces her to the small town of Lone Star, Texas, she's moved to town and is working at the lovely dress store, and things are looking good. Only problem is the Buckley brother she's quietly watched with reluctant sneak peeks. Caleb took her "stand back" warning early on and has done just that while he dances with every female at the town dances. The man obviously enjoys life…but she's not going there.

And yet sometimes life takes a turn and there is no control—and she's about to find that out—but she's going to fight it with all she's got.

Welcome back to the Buckley brothers and their cousins' life in Lone Star…the town full of wonderful, meddling people who suddenly have a new couple to focus on matching up.

Can love overcome despite the reluctance of two people who aren't on the lookout for it?

CHAPTER ONE

Caleb Buckley parked his truck in front of the Mulberry Diner, got out, and glanced over at the dress store next to it, then at Jasmine Scott's car parked a few spaces down from him.

She was inside.

His pulse shifted into a jig, confusing him. Yes, she had his curiosity churning, but he pushed it away as he headed toward the diner's door. The chances of seeing Jasmine here among the lunch rush was likely; he just wasn't sure why that had his attention on high alert.

He was having lunch with his brothers, and a lot of times she would say hi when she came in, but there was a distinct detachment from—maybe not just him, but most—men. Men around her age, men who showed interest. He had watched it. The woman was beautiful with her warm, dark hair and eyes as golden as a setting sun that drew attention. So maybe she'd grown tired of men staring or maybe…something had caused her to be standoffish with men.

Oh, she smiled when she was with the women in town; it was amazing. And she could laugh, too; he'd seen it from a distance. The sound of her laugh sent an electric sizzle through him—not something he was used to. He enjoyed being around ladies but hadn't ever experienced anything that was electric—which was fine with him. He was in *no* rush to find the lifelong relationship that his cousin and other brothers had found. Though he was happy for them, he just wasn't ready.

He enjoyed being single, and he enjoyed the town dances that had become a big draw for their small town. Because of this, they now held them once a month. And since he loved to dance so much, he looked forward to it. He loved dancing almost as much as his younger cousin Ace loved to dance. He knew he wasn't as good as Ace, but it was the fun of taking the gals onto the dance floor and helping them have a good time. A good time was the name of the game.

Lately, because he danced so much, he'd started

being called the Happy Dancin' Cowboy. He thought it was funny and it was actually the truth—when the dance started, he was usually the first on the dance floor and the last off. And tomorrow night would be the same because it was the monthly dance, and he'd be there.

His family owned a humongous ranch, and they had the dollars coming in; they were lucky to have what they had but he didn't take advantage of it. He worked hard and enjoyed working the ranch. Caleb was driven to put in a long day at work; something in him pushed him to do the things he loved, and that was working the ranch and dancing. He used to travel to other towns on the nights he was off to find a dance, but now the town brought the dances to him and he loved it. It wasn't a braggy thing, knowing for a fact that women came from all over the place, looking forward to dancing with him. Word was out.

He figured it was two things. Sadly, one was the fact that he and his brothers were worth a lot of money, and he could always tell when the woman dancing with him had her mind on getting some of those dollars. Oh, he had fun with that too—if they wanted to dance with him just because he was a millionaire, fine, but it never went further than a dance. He wasn't playing around and had no intentions of getting caught in a problem that all he had to do was avoid. He'd learned that lesson early on and could have shut down his love of dancing, holed up and never stepped out on the floor again. But he'd learned how to handle a woman trying to trick him into marrying her. And that was not to go anywhere but the dance floor with them, and he usually figured out after one dance who those gals were, and one dance was the end of it.

Then there were those like him who just loved to dance: there were no attachments, no strings applied. They just liked to get out on that floor, have a good time dancing with a smile and moving to the rhythm of that beat…slow, fast, or whatever. It just made him happy to see someone enjoy it as much as him. Yup, he was, in fact, a happy dancin' cowboy, so the nickname didn't bother him.

And then there was Jasmine, the woman who *never* danced.

Not once since moving to town had she danced. And yup, he'd noticed the fact. He wasn't sure whether that drew his attention after the one time asking her to dance at her first appearance at the town dance. Her reply had been quite frank and firm. And she'd been the first woman to turn him down in a long time.

After that he'd watched her from afar, a lot of times while he was out on the dance floor dancing with somebody else. He'd watched how she mingled with all the gals from the stores and diner: Josie Jane, Ruby, and Millie, the ex-rodeo queen now store owner. And the younger ladies, too. But she seemed drawn to the older ladies, especially Millie. Then again, Millie, until lately, never danced either. Now she danced with Lumas from the fishing store. And they made a great couple and had rumors floating around and hope that maybe the older couple might be having a romance off the dance floor.

He glanced back at the store. His thoughts had gone on a rampage this afternoon, and why, he still wasn't certain. He'd watched a lot of cowboys ask Jasmine to dance and saw them *all* get turned down, just like him. Obviously, the woman did not dance. She had a door slammed down on that so hard that it was impenetrable.

So why did his mind keep going back to her? Why did he wonder what had made her so blunt about having nothing to do with a man?

And, above all else, why was it driving him crazy?

Yup, it was and there was no denying it.

He walked into the diner, and Ruby, the sweet

owner, smiled. "I already have your seat ready." She leaned close. "I saw you glance over at Genna's Classy-Sassy Boutique. Do you like my new outfit? I got it from there."

Caught. He grinned. "You are as dazzling as ever, Mrs. Ruby, so obviously my sister-in-law knows how to stock a great bunch of clothes."

She chuckled. "Yes, she does. And you like dancing, and she made that possible too."

"Yes, ma'am, that's true. I like to dance, and she and all you business owners made it possible for all of us to have a good time."

"We love watching all of you have a good time." She led him to the table by the front window and he sat, as usual, in the booth seat where he had the store next door in sight.

He remembered when his brother, West, used to do that, watching for Genna after she opened the store. He remembered teasing West, along with their other brothers, about it. Now West and Genna were happily married, and they lived on the family farm where his grandparents had lived on the ranch. And they had kept up his grandmother's family history of raising goats when they married. The Buckley Ranch was known mainly for raising cattle and horses, and then goats on the side. West had always loved the goats and took on keeping Grandma's legacy going after their grandparents' passing. He'd lived in their home and continued raising the goats. And, miraculously, when Genna moved to town and opened a dress store, she'd always dreamed of raising goats. And the goats had helped seal the deal of the two falling in love and carrying on the legacy.

It was crazy odd how things worked out sometimes. Genna loved goats; her online business had brought folks in from all over who wanted to have their picture with her put up on her website. And now, they wanted to dance at the well-known end-of-month dance in Lone Star, Texas.

He wasn't complaining. No sir, he wasn't. That dance had brought Jasmine to town and then started this craziness in his head of wondering why she wouldn't dance.

"Would you like something to drink?" Ruby asked, and only then did he realize he'd started staring out the window as she stood, watching him.

"Unsweet tea, please, and I'll decide what I want for lunch when you get back. Always want to know what the special is." He grinned.

"Unsweet tea it is. And we're having, you know, our usual dishes but today my Red is making his special crawfish bowl. You like crawfish, right?"

He laughed. "You know I do. Not everybody does but, yeah, I love it. Grandpa and Grandma passed that on to us. Grams could make some good crawfish, and you and Red do it great justice. So yes, you solved my mystery of what I'm having for lunch. Thank you very much."

Grinning, she tapped him on the shoulder. "You're welcome. And I'm just going to say it right now that I wish you'd try really hard to get that sweet Jasmine on the dance floor tomorrow night. We've all been watching her at all these dances since she came to town, and she hasn't danced yet. You know, her mother, Audrey, came to town to visit Genna's store before anybody. She was the one who put that idea of having the dances in Genna's mind, and that's where all these dances began…that mother wanting to get her daughter here to start a new life.

"And now Jasmine is here, working for Genna, and a wonderful young woman. But getting out on that dance floor is not happening. We're all wondering why.

But what I know is, you, Caleb Buckley, have got magic out on that dance floor."

"Now, I'm not so sure about that." *Where was this going?*

"You know you do. And I saw you ask her out to dance that very first dance she came to, and she said no to you and every cowboy who asked. But I've been watching, and I haven't seen you ask her to dance again."

"She doesn't want to dance." He had a bad feeling growing.

"Maybe, and maybe not. So I'm asking for a favor—I know you like me and hope you'll say yes." She chuckled, her eyes radiant, and he laughed, too, because everybody liked Ruby. "Please ask Jasmine to dance again and try to convince her to get out on that dance floor tomorrow night. All of us ladies agree she needs to begin enjoying herself and not stay holed up with us."

One thing Caleb had never been was nervous, but suddenly he was. He was a sure-footed cowboy and knew whatever he started, he could finish because of his determination. But getting Jasmine on the dance floor was going to be a very complicated task. Not simply because she didn't want to get on the dance floor, but for some reason he couldn't explain, now he was scared to get her on that dance floor with him.

And why is that?

* * *

Jasmine Scott was putting a new outfit on the mannequin near the front window, thankfully not the one in the front window. She'd have been standing there when Caleb Buckley drove up and got out of his truck. His large truck was similar to that of his brothers, but this one had wider tires and stood higher off the ground. *Kind of like Caleb.*

Not a thought she'd meant to think, but ever since she started working at Genna's Classy-Sassy Boutique—after her mother had gotten her here, knowing she could start over here in this lovely little town—she'd been drawn to that cowboy, whether she wanted to be or not. She didn't want to be drawn to anyone. But something about Caleb drew her, and she knew what it was—and that was not good.

She'd taken this job at the boutique and loved it.

She loved all the women in town; she loved everybody, and it was fun, to an extent. Her life before this had been a complete and utter disaster—kind of a nightmare, actually, one she didn't think about often…not anymore since moving here.

Fact was she had no desire to start another relationship.

And she knew the ladies had their eyes on her. But no dating, nothing that had to do with another relationship—if that was what she could call the last calamity that had ruined her desire to ever try that again.

She loved this town despite the fact that it was packed with cowboys. She enjoyed seeing cowboys; she just had no desire to *date* a cowboy ever again. She liked going to the monthly dances and watching everybody have a blast. There had been a time where she had loved dancing herself, but no more.

No more.

Her gaze went to the window of the store and Caleb's truck. She rubbed her temple. She always noticed Caleb's gigantic truck, *always* noticed after dancing with every woman he asked at the dances that he always left alone. And as much as she wanted nothing about him to appeal to her, that did…

Maybe *appeal* wasn't the right word—*curious* was better.

She wondered whether he had had an experience that made "dating shenanigans" a no-go there. Wondered if he'd had a disastrous experience like she'd had?

Stop. She focused on getting the clothes on the mannequin and not the fact that Caleb was next door at the diner where she would be eating soon. She got the skirt on the mannequin just as another truck pulled up next door and she saw two of his brothers and one of his cousins get out. Ryder, Zack, and Hunter climbed from their truck. Goodness, just like Caleb, they were tall, broad-shouldered, and handsome. They looked great, despite the fact that they wore faded work jeans and muddied boots that they all three stomped briefly on the pavement before stepping onto the sidewalk. She liked that they'd tried to clean up before entering the diner. Caleb would have done that, too, but he didn't have muddy boots. Obviously, they had been doing separate work jobs on the ranch today and were now meeting for lunch.

"Okay, I'm done. Are you ready for lunch?" Genna Buckley called as she came from the back room. "I'll turn the sign. I'm really hungry today." She smiled at Jasmine as she walked to the door.

Jasmine didn't want to go over there right now. All three of the Buckleys who'd just walked past were single, handsome men, and yet she didn't have any extra thoughts about them. Just Caleb. He was the one who bothered her. He was the one she always tried to avoid. Thankfully, he had asked her to dance once and had taken her *no, thank you* sincerely and had since left her alone, which made her happy. However, sometimes, whether she wanted to or not, she woke up in the middle of the night imagining she was out there, showing Caleb that she could dance. And dance as well as he could. Nope, nada—she wasn't showing anybody that, not ever again.

"Lunch time, workaholic." Genna chuckled from the open door.

She shot her gaze to Genna. "I'm sorry. I was,

umm, lost in thought. I'm ready too."

Ready or not, she had to go. Thankfully, she'd gotten the mannequin changed and nothing fell off. Her insides were diving off a cliff right now as she walked outside and waited for her boss—her good friend—to lock up behind them. Then they walked the short few feet to Mulberry Diner.

And, of course, as she had already assumed, the Buckley brothers sat by the front window, and her gaze instantly latched onto Caleb's. She yanked her gaze away and entered the door Genna held open. *Why?* This was a large diner; it had several booths near the window, and of all of those there, she'd locked gazes with Caleb.

Ruby Mulberry, the sweet owner, and her husband, Red, were wonderful. The man could beat anyone at cooking. His food drew people to this town, and they usually packed the place at breakfast and lunch and sometimes dinner. Ruby, she loved the Buckleys, and always made certain there was a booth open at the window for them. Why, because one or all of them was going to show up and they liked the window view, so Ruby made sure to save a spot for them.

"Well, good morning. I thought you gals would be coming to eat. I'm sure you're gearing up for the weekend crowd with the dance coming tomorrow. They're already arriving, as you can tell," she glanced around the quickly filling diner. "Jasmine, I heard from Sydney that your family has her B&B all booked up this weekend and will start arriving this afternoon."

"Yes, ma'am. They're excited about the dancing and shopping they'll be doing." Her mom and tons of her family always kept Sydney and Dustin Buckley and sweet little Hazel's large bed-and-breakfast filled up on the weekend of the dance. She was thankful that the little cabin she rented was farther out in the country. Yes, she rented a cabin at the far end of a section of the Buckley Ranch, and thankfully it was small. It was a place she could hide out, and be alone, more importantly it was far too small for her family to come and stay for the dances. Thankfully her mom always had a great time at the bed-and-breakfast, so Jasmine didn't feel bad about her place being too small.

She would go over for a visit after they arrived, and she would go back to the cabin alone. She found peace at her cabin, a peace that she needed.

Peace wasn't surrounding her as Ruby led them to the booth with its back connected to the one where the Buckleys sat. Before she could take the seat that would put her back to Caleb, Genna slid into that side, which meant Jasmine had a direct view of Caleb, and he of her.

Caleb wasn't the most outstandingly good-looking of the Buckley brothers; they were all handsome in their own ways but Caleb had sandier brown hair, not the black hair that most of them had. He had olive-green eyes and a smile, oh goodness, a smile that at that moment lit up as he looked at her.

Her heart instantly blew up in a rampage of thundering palpitations. *How, oh how, was she going to spend this whole lunchtime with him right there in her vision?* And eating was out—the last thing she needed was to choke on something, and him have to squeeze it out of her. But there it was; he was smiling and, with absolutely no other option, she smiled back.

CHAPTER TWO

Jasmine had returned his smile—well, at least her lips had lifted at the edges slightly.

"Hi, fellas." Genna turned and looked over the booth at Caleb, Ryder, Zack, and Hunter. "Great to see all of you. I just talked to West, and he and that sweet niece, Hazel, have made it to San Marcos with the load of sweet baby goats."

Everyone said hello to their sister-in-law, and Caleb's gaze locked onto Jasmine, who now looked uncomfortable, as usual. He shifted to Genna. "He likes delivering those goats to kids who really want them to show at their county livestock shows. I think he wants to be Santa Claus."

Genna chuckled. "I think you've called it right."

Ryder said, "On that, he took after Grandma."

Hunter and Zack agreed. Caleb did, too, but his gaze went back to the quiet Jasmine.

There was no denying that Jasmine Scott was beautiful. Not that she enjoyed looking at him. Nope, there was always that shutter that dropped over those amazing golden eyes of hers when she looked at him. *Why?* He let the question slide as his eyes dug into hers, and he saw a flicker in their golden depths. Obviously, she wasn't thrilled to have to look at him across the booth, probably wishing she was sitting where Genna was sitting and able to turn her back on him. But he had a splendid view of her, and he smiled again, just to see her reaction. Her eyes shot away instantly and then came back to his, which he liked. He widened the grin into a smile when he saw her slam down the shutters as she glanced down at her menu.

"Are you ready for the dance, Jasmine?" he asked directly, causing her to have to look up and meet his gaze.

"I'm going to help with refreshments like always," she said, no emotion in her words.

"Maybe you'll dance this time." He couldn't help

it. Ruby's words stuck in his mind as Jasmine's golden gaze dimmed and two vertical lines appeared between her eyebrows.

"No, I don't dance. But I like visiting with everyone."

"Maybe you should try. It's not hard. I could show you."

Those beautiful eyes flashed. "No. I'll stay on the side, helping out."

That was a frank shutdown, but he saw Genna and his brothers take notice of it too, and so he carried on. "You do help keep everyone fed or hydrated at the dances. But it's time for you to have a little fun. It's not like you don't get asked by a ton of cowboys."

Her jaw tensed. "That's nice of you and them, but I'll stay *off* of the dance floor."

What was it with her and not dancing? Maybe she had no rhythm or something like that, but he didn't think so. He was suddenly completely challenged to try to change her mind. To see where it led…

Trouble, it could very well lead to trouble.

But looking into those eyes of hers, he knew he was

going in anyway. Trouble or no trouble, he wanted Jasmine on the dance floor with him.

* * *

"You were quiet in the diner."

Jasmine looked at her friend. "I'm quiet a lot."

"I've noticed that, especially when my brother-in-law Caleb is around. He's a really nice guy."

Jasmine wished a customer would walk in. "He is a very nice guy. I can't deny that, and he's a great dancer—"

"And he wants to dance with you."

"Yes, but I don't dance, so I hope all of you little cheerleaders at the dances don't think that's going to happen, because it's not."

Genna walked over with a vibrant red blouse in her hand. It was a beautiful silk T-shirt, and she handed it to Jasmine. "I think you should wear this. It will be perfect with some of your white jeans and maybe that pretty red pair of leather flats that you own."

Jasmine wanted to roll her eyes, but this was her

friend and boss. "I hope you're just telling me that so I can wear it and help sell clothes here at the store."

Genna chuckled. "*That* is exactly what I'm trying to do—you're going to wear it for free, and hopefully we're going to get customers in because of how stunning you make it look." She waved toward the rack of the silk T-shirts in various colors. "You're my advertisement because of how fantastic you'll look wearing it. Women will ask where you bought it and you'll tell them."

Jasmine sighed. "You know I'm a sucker for beautiful clothes and my mother is too. But many others come to town just for this store and your super taste so *many* women at the dance will be wearing clothing from this store. Which means me wearing a red silk T-shirt is not going to be a big deal."

"I think it is. You're going to stand out, and when you get out on the dance floor—if you would dance— you'll help me advertise the store better. I'll have the announcer say, 'Look at the stunning Jasmine, wearing one of Genna's Sassy-Classy Boutique's amazing T-shirts.'"

Jasmine laughed—wishing she'd groaned instead. "You are hilarious. But, Mr. Lumas can announce that Jasmine, standing over there by the drink table, can give you any type of soda, lemonade made by our own Josie Jane, or a diet drink, or a glass of water, and while doing so, notice she's wearing an outstanding red T-shirt from Genna's Classy-Sassy Boutique."

Genna reached out and wrapped her arms around Jasmine in a hug. "I guess I can't entice you to go out on the floor and advertise for me because, yes, if I really ask Lumas to advertise my T-shirts like that, he would. And he'd find you wherever you were and give me a shout-out. But, that might be a good idea now that you've said it's okay, because he can point you out so Caleb or some of the other fellas will know where you are to ask you to dance."

A lot of men had asked her to dance at the town dance, and she had told all of them no, she didn't dance. She didn't stress to them that she would never, *ever* dance again, but that was what was going on in her mind each time she was asked.

Still, looking at Genna, she knew her friend's heart was in a good place, trying to help Jasmine overcome something in her background. And though Jasmine didn't talk about it, she knew many of the ladies in town had picked up on that about her. They had never pushed her to talk. Every once in a while, she'd let a few see a little deeper. Millie Watts was one of those when she'd talked to Sydney, Genna's sister-in-law now; but at that time, Sydney had been uncertain about remarrying after losing her first love and the father of sweet Hazel. Millie had also lost her husband and never remarried, but that night she'd opened up to urge Sydney to not hold back.

Hearing both speak of their deep love and loss had struck Jasmine hard, and she'd tried to talk herself into overcoming her past. Her hurt didn't compare to theirs; hers was about her lack of brains—at least that was how she looked at it. She'd *thought* she had love, been blinded by that thought and didn't realize she had betrayal. Now, she didn't trust herself to ever take that chance again. Especially since she was in a happy place here in Lone Star.

A happy place she didn't want to mess up.

Genna had had her own struggles, and Jasmine knew she'd overcome them for love, and of course they were hoping she could too. They didn't know she was never going to date again.

"I don't want to dance, and I won't." She met Genna's gaze with eyes she hoped showed her determined mindset on the subject. "Look, the main goal for these dances is to have fun and, so you know, I have a blast standing over there by all those older ladies of Lone Star. They are amazing and funny. I'm having fun with them. I've really enjoyed watching Millie loosen up after years of not dancing. Last time, she danced with Lumas, while I oversaw the drink table, and I hope she'll dance with him tomorrow night, knowing I'll be there to watch her table."

Genna crossed her arms and leaned her head to the side, her eyes penetrating Jasmine's. "You're right. Millie lost her husband in that horrible rodeo accident, and after she and Lumas helped match his granddaughter and Ace up, they've started dancing. And it looks like they're loving it. Jasmine, that could be *you.* I simply wanted you to know that sometimes to make a difference in your past, you have to take a step forward. Maybe, just maybe, tomorrow you could step out and dance one dance. Just one. But that's it from me, no more pushing. It's your decision." She smiled, then walked away.

Relief swarmed over Jasmine that her friend would now let her be. She turned and looked out the window to the main street where the setup was already ready for the dance. Lights were up, tubs of flowers were all about, and tomorrow tables would be set up. The band would start playing at seven, and everyone would come from all over, her mom included.

And she would stand behind the table and enjoy the show from there. Others had done it too, until they found the man they wanted…now everyone was hoping Millie and Lumas were slowly, carefully finding their way to new beginnings.

Why had her brain gone there? Yes, others had stood there behind that table beside wonderful Millie, a woman who had never danced before because she had been hurt and just couldn't let herself have fun, and now she seemed to be enjoying herself. But no matter how much anybody wanted Jasmine to get out there, it wasn't happening.

* * *

"Caleb, I'm not surprised that you're here early," West said as Caleb walked up to the dance area.

"I'm *always* here early, and you know it." He grinned, everyone knew it was true. "Anything I can help do?"

His brother hitched a brow. "Sure, you can help by continuing to make certain that all the lovely ladies who come to this dance have somebody to dance with at some point in the evening. We know we can always count on you for that."

"You know me well. I'm always happy to help, so you can count on me to continue taking care of that." He looked across the setup and caught a view of Jasmine as she talked with Ruby and Josie Jane as the group of older ladies who sat in chairs and knitted or crocheted while enjoying the dance and visiting began to gather. And some of them danced, too. They were always near the refreshments so they could visit with everyone as they came off the dance floor for refreshments. He tried not to stare but the woman did draw his attention.

"I see you still have your eyes on Jasmine."

He looked at West, who had not just a grin but a "I know you're interested" grin.

He crashed his brows together. "I just happened to look over there."

"Sure, deny it all you want, but we all suspect that our brother, who dates many, has a constant spark in his eyes when it comes to Jasmine. I heard from Ruby that she asked you to get Jasmine on the dance floor." He grinned. "Sounds like you are getting ready for a show."

"A show? No way." He was startled that Ruby was telling people he had agreed to get Jasmine on the dance floor. "Ruby asked me that and I told her I would, but Jasmine has a mind of her own. She doesn't dance; it doesn't go unnoticed by anyone. Honestly, when I asked her that first time, like I ask every lady, she was pretty blunt…like, *no way* was she going to dance. So, in all honesty, again, I'm not sure if she has a problem with dancing or a problem with men. She only talks to men in her age range if she has to. Something is up with that."

"You've really been watching, checking her out, and storing it up like it's a puzzle to be solved, brother."

Caleb snatched his hat off and rammed his fingers from his forehead, through his hair, and onto his now tense neck. "Look, I'm going to try because Ruby asked me to, *and* I think everyone knows something had to have happened to make Jasmine so standoffish. So, it's a combination of curiosity about why she's like that, mixed with concern, and it's a challenge."

"And everyone knows you like a challenge." West grinned, then grew serious. "We're all seeing what you've described. Genna has purposely given her space but I can tell she's worried and thinks getting on the dance floor might be good for her. So what are you going to do?"

"I'm going to ask her to dance. But if she says no, then everyone needs to give her space. It is, after all, her choice. No one else's."

"You're right about that. I think everyone is just glad you're going to give it a shot. That you're up for the challenge. Right?"

Challenge it was, more than anyone knew.

You're not up for the challenge. He wasn't pleased with the voice in his head. He liked to think he was up for any challenge but for some reason, the beautiful Jasmine had him not so sure.

Was he not up for the challenge? He didn't know, but he would try to figure out tonight what about her and her telling him no caused him so much uncertainty.

He hadn't been turned down for dances in a very long time but he knew it wouldn't faze him if he was because he'd just asked somebody else. But as his brother looked at him and waited for an answer, he knew there was just something different about Jasmine saying no.

He didn't know whether her "no" had to do with

him or had to do with something else, something from her past. And if it was from her past, then maybe he needed to dig a little deeper to find out why.

Why that thought kept plaguing him in the back of his brain, he wasn't sure, but tonight he would try to get her on the dance floor. "I did promise Ruby that I would, but all you folks who are pushing me to do this need to understand that sometimes when a woman says no, there's a reason for it. If Jasmine doesn't want to dance, that's her business, not anybody else's. She can say no as many times as she wants. And the fact is that it doesn't matter how many times somebody asks her; she can say no again until everyone finally gets the hint that she doesn't want to dance."

His brother's eyes turned serious. "Yeah, you're right. You're absolutely right. And I think that's great you made that statement. You'll hold to it. Maybe she needs someone like you to stand in there and tell people to butt out."

"One thing I noticed about Jasmine is she doesn't mind saying what she means, not always in words but sometimes in her attitude, and other times she leaves quietly. But I do know that first time she came to the dance and I asked her to dance, she made it clear the answer was no. I got the message. She does it quite well and, in all honesty, with grace. She didn't say anything ugly; she just told me no quite firmly. So who knows what tonight will bring? Stay tuned, brother."

West gave him a squeeze to his shoulder. "I know you—you'll figure it out. And now you've got me thinking you could be completely right. I also know if she has a problem and she needs help, you're the guy to help her. I think Ruby must think that too. All right, I've got to go. It looks like the band will be starting soon, so good luck, dude."

He watched his brother walk away, his mind spinning with the thoughts he'd shut down when they would surface. But as he watched how Jasmine communicated well with women, he knew something truly wasn't right.

She laughed out loud at something one of the ladies said, and around women, she did that. But when a man was around, she was standoffish, like yesterday. It wasn't any of his business, but still…it was on his mind and that's where he had a problem. When something wasn't right, he was the cowboy who couldn't walk away. It would be on his mind until he figured out why.

So, he could be heading into trouble. But backing down wasn't something he did. What would be, would be, and *that* was *that*.

CHAPTER THREE

Jasmine stood beside the drink table, passing out sodas and homemade lemonades, watching as everybody had a great time. Singles, families— everyone was enjoying the beautiful summer night. And the band was very good, able to sing top hits and oldies as well.

Her gaze lingered where it shouldn't whether she wanted it to or not as Caleb, in his usual, talented way, danced the early part of the night away. It had only been about forty minutes since the dance had officially begun. And as usual, he was out there instantly, with a smiling woman. She was his eighth partner, and they'd smiled as if they were in heaven or had won the lottery.

Right now, he was spinning her to his other side, under his arm as she twirled; they two-stepped along with the music. It was just very graceful; both of them knew what they were doing and were creative. She watched him grin as the woman laughed while twirling under his raised arm again. Then he pulled her close before twirling her out away from his hug.

Jasmine remembered those days she and her partner danced like that.

She didn't want to but watching Caleb, she always saw talent, inspiration, and most of all, heart.

She had watched him since moving here and saw that he had wonderful talent but also recognized the talent of the woman dancing with him. That had drawn her to begin watching him…well, his mesmerizing eyes had drawn her first, and she'd quickly shot that down. But it was his ability to always give the woman he danced with a good time while he made sure he didn't over dance them or under dance them. He always developed his dance to match theirs and helped them do a little bit better than they would have done without him. She admired that about Caleb, whether she wanted to or not.

The man was good, and she had yet to see any

woman he danced with not be smiling when they finished and he went to his next partner. She realized the man hardly ever looked as though he was dating anyone in particular.

Not that she wanted to notice that, but it was fairly apparent. She was not interested, and yet she couldn't deny that she was curious about him. As the dance ended, she saw one of the children approaching her table and, glad to have something else to do other than watch the man she needed not to watch, she smiled at the boy. "Are you looking for something to drink?"

"Yes, ma'am. I hear the lemonade's really great, so can I have a glass?"

"You heard right. Josie Jane from the store right across the street there always makes it and believe me, there is none better than hers." She filled a paper cup with ice, then poured the wonderful homemade, fresh from ripe lemons, lemonade into the glass and then handed it to the little boy. As the kid said thank you and hurried off, her eyesight caught on Caleb, who was now walking her way.

He was literally dancing the night away and had to

be thirsty. She was watching the table alone because Millie had been out there dancing with Lumas. Those two were great on the dance floor together and, like everybody in town, she hoped there was a romance growing between them. She used that thought as a distraction as Caleb reached her.

"I see you're handing out awesome drinks to make people smile. That little boy was grinning while drinking that lemonade as he walked away." She gave him a small smile, making sure to keep it slight. "Yes, you know who made that, and you know it's always undeniably the best lemonade in the world."

"That's for sure. I see that Millie is heading back after her dance with Lumas and so the table will be watched, so how about a dance? It's fun and you watch everyone else with interest. Why not give it a try?"

Steam rolled inside her. He knew she always said no. "I already told you once I'm not going to dance. I'll be honest—you're a great dancer, and I like the way that you treat everybody. I see that if the lady isn't the best dancer, you make sure she feels like she is, and that takes talent, you know."

He crossed his arms and cocked his head to the side. "So you watch me dancing. You noticed that? Not everyone does."

What had she done, opening her big mouth? "I watch everyone dancing, and I noticed your last dancer wasn't the best in the world but you taught her some moves. You made sure she learned them without realizing she was truly learning them from you. You're great about that."

That amazing grin of his spread across his handsome face. "Well, I'll be. You are *very* observant. Yeah, I can tell when somebody doesn't really know how to dance the best in the world, and I'm not going to tell them they're not any good. I mean, I've got them out there—why not try to help them learn a little better? And honestly, then I feel good when I look out and see them dancing better with somebody else."

Her heart squeezed at his words. His gaze lingered on her, and she knew that she had said too much. *But what else could she say now?*

"Obviously you have watched me dancing and realized that about the people I'm dancing with, so that means you know a lot about dancing.”

“Look, just because I don’t dance now doesn’t mean I haven’t ever danced.” *Why had she said* that!

“Exactly what I thought. So, come on, just come on out here and dance with me one time. You’d make a lot of people happy if you did that, you know.”

“I don’t dance.”

His eyes twinkled and his grin did a number on her pounding pulse.

“All the wonderful older ladies in town are thinking you don’t dance because you don’t know how, or that you’re afraid for some strange reason. They don’t realize—and I didn’t, either—that you obviously do know how. So now you have my curiosity up, and I can’t help but wonder…how good can you spin? Come on, show me and make a lot of people happy.”

“I—”

A grin spread across his face, broad and wide, and he held his hand out to her. “Come on. Come on, dance with me. I promise you that I won’t think much about it. It’s not a commitment or anything crazy like that.” He chuckled.

And so did Millie as she walked up and heard his words. "Yes, go dance with Caleb." She came behind the table and the tall cowgirl took Jasmine's arm and pulled her forward.

"No, I—"

"Yes," Millie said. "Do it for me. I really want to see you get out there and have some fun. Believe me, you know you started standing beside me here at my table because I refused to get out there. But now I'm out there some and really enjoy it. Everybody who doesn't want to dance stands beside me behind this table and that's about to stop." She grinned widely. "No more watching from behind my table. I can tell you that I've loved getting back out there and hope you will too."

She didn't say she was enjoying dancing with only one man, but Jasmine knew it. Jasmine looked from Millie to Caleb and sighed. Her heart thundered like a raging storm. Taking a breath, she lifted her hand and placed it into Caleb's. "Okay, I'll do it. But one dance doesn't mean I'll be getting out here all the time anymore." It wasn't a question—it was a "You get it?".

They both smiled as she looked from Millie to Caleb, the man holding her hand and making her heart pound as if she were racing from a wildfire.

And she basically was. Oh boy, was she.

* * *

Caleb couldn't help grinning as he held Jasmine's hand in his and led her as they crossed toward the dance floor. He didn't look from side to side, but kept his gaze down as he led her to the dancing area. He still didn't look at her as he towed her behind him, not wanting to give her a chance to shake her head and change her mind. She kept up as he led her toward the middle of the dance floor so they were surrounded, keeping her more in his space versus having an easy out on the edges to turn and walk away if she got the impulse to do so. Once they were where he wanted, he turned toward her, keeping her hand in his, very aware of heat sparking from her fingers to his. The touch of her soft hand to his was nothing like he'd ever experienced.

Something he was not going to focus on at the moment.

No, it was that strong, defiant look in her eyes when his gaze connected with hers that startled him. *Was that a challenge?*

Surely not. He grinned. "So, you up for this dance?"

"I'm out here."

He laughed at her and the fact that the band started to play the Dierks Bentley song, "What Was I Thinkin'." He glanced at them and the lead singer; Jess, grinned at him as he belted out the song. The only thing wrong was Caleb knew what he was thinking. "Can you swing?" He tugged her in and then spun her out and caught the beat—and she did too. Her gaze snapped to his, and she never missed a moment as the song, humorous in its words, went on. But wow, this woman could dance.

The rhythm was meant for fun, and he and Jasmine swung as if they'd been dancing together forever. He couldn't help grinning as he pulled her past him and spun toward her, watching the spirit of the dance in her moves. There were others dancing along with them, but he felt like it was just the two of them, eyes locked as he challenged her, and she took him up on it as if it were a slip and slide on the playground.

He couldn't help it; he spun her, then took her into a dip so he was holding her parallel to the ground. He looked down into those sparkling golden eyes that for a minute had nothing but happiness in them. Something he'd never seen in her eyes until that moment, and he grinned at her. To his complete surprise, she smiled back up at him as he pulled her up. *She knew how to dance.*

Not only that, the twinkle in her eyes was as if she'd just gotten a new life. Still holding her fingers in his hands, he pulled her close and looked down into her eyes. "You dance like magic."

Her expression shifted instantly into an unreadable gaze. "Yes, like I told you, I never said I couldn't dance. I just don't."

He spun her away and pulled her back. This time, their bodies touched momentarily as he let her pass in the other direction. He watched her do her steps away from him and then realized they had been getting into the dance so well together that people had parted, and now they were in the center of the dance floor, surrounded by couples no longer dancing but watching them with smiles.

Unable to help himself, he spun her widely then back into his arms and dipped her as they came together. Then, once he tugged her back up, he pulled her around and unable to help himself, leaned her back once more and looking into her sparkling eyes, his breath caught as she held his gaze. Heart pounding he pulled her up against him before spinning her away—and now unsurprising to him, Caleb watched the beauty never miss a step.

Jasmine knew exactly what they were doing in this dance. It was a dance that could be taken one step at a time or turned into a free-for-all of two people who knew how to do it and keep rhythm with the song while having fun with each other. And he'd had fun, was having fun, and *that* was for certain.

"Are you having as much fun as I am?" he asked as they once again touched and he shifted one hand to the other.

"Yes, I am." She spun away, and he hung on to her fingers, wanting more…wanting to hold her close.

As the song ended, he did what he'd wanted and drew her close. "Don't leave. Dance with me on the next dance." They were standing there in the middle as suddenly everyone around them started to clap. "You dance amazingly. And that was just our first dance. You've got a crowd watching. Come on—stay for another dance."

Her eyes looked suddenly troubled. "I haven't done that in a very, very long time, and I did enjoy it. But don't expect anything."

Don't expect anything? "I'm not. I just want to dance with you. I want to see what you can do, because you definitely know what you are doing."

People were telling them to dance again as the band had started a new song. This time, it was a slow dance. But slow dances could be exciting, with more moves than just two-stepping around the room, and he had a feeling she knew this too.

He grinned. "The music's started and everybody's watching, so let's do this again."

She sighed. "One more then, Mr. Slow Stepper. I've watched you…I know you know what you're doing."

He grinned and drew her close, but not too close. His arm rested at her lower back; his other hand held her arm out beside his. And then he stepped forward; she stepped back, and the dance began. They two-stepped around the room with everybody and then he spun her out and spun her back to him, and she was smiling.

"I've watched you…I know you know what you're doing." Her words trickled through him.

And then he dipped her. He didn't want to pull her back up; he just wanted to hold her there in his arms, looking down into her eyes. He wanted to kiss her right then and there. No doubt about it, he had not felt this before, dancing with anyone. He missed a beat because he was still holding her down in that position, and he knew everybody watching knew he had missed his beat. She shifted, so he stood back up and pulled her with him. There was that glance again, but he knew something was different and she didn't like it.

* * *

Jasmine had lost it. As he had held her dipped down, his arm beneath her back and his gaze locked to hers, her heart pounded with the music's rhythm. He lifted her back up and they continued the slow dance, while her heart went on a rampage of beats. She had missed dancing.

She had closed it off when she had closed her heart from the pain that falling in love with her dance partner had caused.

Falling in love dancing for not just his heart, but winning top country dance championships with him. Only to find out that he'd used her just to win and that his heart was not locked in like hers.

As this dance with Caleb ended, she saw that look in Caleb's eyes—that look that told her he knew they just danced two fantastic dances.

And he knew something wasn't right. The song ended and clapping erupted, along with cheers, with everyone wanting them to dance again. She shook her head and managed a smile at everybody; then, not really knowing what else to do, she turned and walked away. Thank goodness Caleb let loose of her fingers. The tingle that had been radiating up through that touch lingered and stayed as she walked through the open crowd. She didn't head back to the beverage table, but down the street where her car was parked. She needed to go home.

She needed to be alone, to get her head back on straight, and to push the love of dancing out of the way again.

Never should she have let this happen. She had known just getting out on that dance floor could be dangerous. What she hadn't realized was, getting out on that dance floor with Caleb, who knew how to dance, who knew—whether he even realized it or not—that they had danced well together, with more practice, they could win a championship in a country dance competition.

Oh goodness, she had made a huge mistake.

*It's not just that…*the voice in her brain called out as she stepped harder and harder toward the end of the road, so thankful now that it was darker and there weren't a lot of eyes to watch her. She reached her car at last, relief pouring through her. Caleb wasn't just a good dancer; he was an amazing guy. And despite not wanting him to, he appealed to her—appealed to *all* women; it was clear by the lineup of women wanting to dance with him. But she wasn't going there—she had also thought that Ray was a good guy too, and oh, how wrong she'd been.

She fumbled with her keys, pulling them out of her purse. She had gotten it in the lock when she heard a step behind her. She swung around and there stood Caleb.

"I didn't mean to do something to upset you," he said gently.

Did she look that upset? She turned away. "It's not you. You did nothing wrong. And I'd be a liar if I didn't tell you that you're an amazing dancer."

"Me? *You* are the amazing dancer. You didn't miss a step. I switched up and you immediately caught on. You were made to dance."

She couldn't look at him so she fumbled with her keys.

"You've seen me dance," he continued. "With people who are new and people who are fairly good, but you…you did what I do—you adjusted for me. I have a feeling you could have put me to shame." He laughed.

Her pulse rose and she crossed her arms, staring hard at her feet, then giving up the fight, she looked at him, totally not sure what to do as his deep-olive eyes locked onto her.

She sighed. "I used to love to dance. You found that out tonight. Yes, I can basically do anything, but I can't go back to doing that again. And I can't—I don't want to tell you why, but I have my reasons."

He took a step toward her but stopped. There were about four steps between them; he was giving her space, and she realized that.

Was she like that? Was she a frightened woman who needed space?

Her stomach churned at the idea. "Caleb, you dance wonderful. You are so very talented, and you have such a contagious good time, too. No wonder they've recently gave you that nickname the Happy Dancin' Cowboy…" She chuckled. "…because it's true—you actually are a dancing cowboy and very *happy* about it. And you've also convinced me to get back out there, and I haven't been on a dance floor in—well, never mind. For what it's worth, I had fun, so thanks… Just, um, just don't expect it again, okay?"

He had both hands on his hips now. He was a lean-hipped, wide-shouldered, muscular standout. He was amazing, whether she wanted to admit it or not. It was undeniable. "I've got to go."

"But the dance has barely started and you usually love staying around."

"I really need to go, so go have fun. Do your usual dance with every woman and make them feel like this is the greatest dance around. Make them want to come back. Half of them will come back just to dance with you again. So, don't let me mess that up. It helps the town."

His eyes darkened but his lips curved up. "I just get out there and dance because I like to."

"No, really, you help the town. Half those girls do come back from all over the state. They want to dance with *you*—you're good, really good and nice too. And…a lot of them are probably challenged by the fact that you don't seem to take anybody home with you."

Why had she said that? What had possessed her to go there?

His expression changed…not to anger but to something else as he realized that she watched him. "I don't. I come here to dance, and that's *all.* I've *never* taken anybody home with me."

Why was he telling her that?

Because you started it!

They were barely friends, barely knew each other— she rarely spoke to him and he knew it, so why had she even gone there? It was his personal business and none of hers.

"Good night," she forced out. "And whether I want to say it or not, thanks for the two dances. They were wonderful." Then, without hesitating, she sank into her car and closed the door.

And, as usual, he didn't pursue her. He was a man who asked you to dance; if you said no, he moved away and asked the next one. And obviously he did that in other things, too—like now, she drove away and he didn't ask her not to.

CHAPTER FOUR

"You're not dancing. What's up?" Hunter asked as he came to stand beside Caleb on the opposite side of the dance than most everybody else.

Caleb looked at his cousin, feeling down. He had remained on the side of the street where he had followed Jasmine to her car. After watching her drive away, he'd headed back to the dance but hadn't made it to the crowd. Instead, he'd stopped near a roadblock for vehicles that they used on the nights of the dance. "Yeah, I'm kind of not in the mood."

"I've got to tell you, we all thought Jasmine might have never danced before since we'd not witnessed it but, man, were we wrong. She was something."

"Something else. The gal can dance—probably the best dancer I've ever danced with. It's amazing. She didn't miss a beat. She even—well, she knew what she was doing."

"You met your match. Why are you looking so down? You looked like you were having more fun out there than I've ever seen you have before."

"You're right. I had a blast. I could dance with her forever, I think. I mean…" He paused. "I didn't mean that like it sounded. I think she would be a great dance partner but obviously she has a different opinion than that. You know what I mean…she doesn't seem like a partner is something she's interested in."

"Everybody's got that opinion, but you did something nobody else has done. You know how many guys have asked her to dance and she has said no to everyone. But this time she danced with you—we don't even know why she doesn't like to dance. We thought she couldn't dance but obviously we were all wrong."

"But look, Hunter, I followed her out to her car and something was wrong. I could tell. She actually told me she had a good time and she enjoyed getting out there but she won't do it again, ever. So what's up with that? What would drive somebody who loves something and enjoys it, is amazing at it, to say never again?"

Hunter looked down at the ground and then lifted his gaze up to meet Caleb's. "You never know. I don't get out there and dance much anymore, and I used to love it. My mom was an amazing dancer, as you know, and I'm not kidding, Caleb—you're good like she was. And I was stunned by Jasmine. Wow, if Mom and Dad were alive, they'd have been right out there beside y'all, kicking it up." He smiled, his eyes bright. "I'd have been watching in awe. Yeah, my incredible mom taught me everything I know about dancing. It was one of our favorite things to do when I was little, before me and Ace lost them in that plane crash. But now, I can't enjoy it. I've tried a few times but something's missing. Ace was the same way, you know, and then Kelsy came along and now they're out there too."

"I'm really sorry about that. Maybe when the right woman comes along like she did for Ace, you'll find that rhythm again."

"Maybe. Anyway, enough about me. I'm just letting you know sometimes when you have something you love, something can happen and change that, no matter how much you still love it. I still love coming to the dances. I think about my mom every time instead of thinking about the girl I'm holding in my arms; I'm thinking about the mom I loved and lost, the mom who taught me to dance. Not exactly what I'm supposed to be thinking… Maybe something happened in Jasmine's life that's now keeping her off the dance floor. But she got out there with you. She did two dances with you, so that might mean something."

Caleb felt so sorry for his younger cousin; he and his brother had been through so much, losing their mom and dad, and he knew that that loss left an emptiness in them. And he also knew Hunter might have hit the mark. "I'm going to think about this, because you might be right. Something is keeping her off that dance floor. It's none of my business, and I should keep my nose out of it like she asked. However, I'm going to try but I can't promise anything. I just need to see if I can help her."

"You can, I think. You connected with her, and you've never looked as happy out there as you looked with her, despite how much you're on the dance floor. You clearly enjoy teaching ladies how to dance. I'm used to that; my mom taught me, it was great from when I knew nothing to knowing so much—and yeah, you do that. You ask the ones who don't know how to dance well and the ones who do know how to dance well, and you're just good with all of them. But tonight." He grinned and it made Caleb feel good—his cousin, after all this talk that they had been doing and how deep it went for Hunter, he was still smiling. *"Tonight*, you found a good challenge and you want to dance again with her, not with somebody else. And that's why you're not out there, huh?"

Bingo. "You, Hunter, are one smart cookie. And I'm in one deep hole right now."

Hunter's smile widened. "Well, now we're going to get out of the sad note here and move on to the happy note. I would see what you could do, see how you can help her because if you don't, you're always going to wonder. Don't let that go." Hunter put a hand on his shoulder and squeezed, and then he walked away.

Caleb stood there and watched him go, knowing that his cousin had hit the mark. Caleb wasn't going to let it go. He just had to figure out how to do it without running the beautiful Jasmine off.

* * *

Sunday morning, Jasmine woke early, having barely slept. She had times like that; it irritated her but then again, she was very grateful she didn't have anything worse than sleep problems. She made coffee, then went outside to the seating area to watch the rising sun. She loved the seating area of the cabin, with its openness to sunrise and sunset. She sat in the red iron chair with the floral cushions that she'd added to them and took a sip of her black coffee.

The sunrise was a combination of soft blue melting into the soft pink, glowing as it rose; then the line of gold appeared and lifted up as she sipped her coffee and enjoyed watching it. A bright-orange sun rose slowly. It was so beautiful, spreading across that pasture. A pasture she had not yet explored. There had come a time after her trouble and her time of becoming a person who wanted to be alone that she had begun to hike a little bit, so maybe she would do that. It was just a pasture, after all, with trees edging the far side of it. She might get back into hiking; maybe it would help get her mind off the thoughts that had to do with Caleb.

That was why she hadn't slept. Plain and simple. She couldn't deny that she had thoroughly enjoyed dancing with him last night. But that didn't mean she was going to keep doing it. She had not been in a relationship since her huge mess-up with her dance partner. What a hideous ordeal. He had been in her thoughts about dancing and the disaster of a horrible relationship. But now thinking about dancing was confusing because there was that handsome Caleb.

She sighed, then took a drink of hot coffee, letting it burn its way down her throat and wake up her brain.

She'd stopped dancing because her dance partner she'd gotten engaged to and thought she loved had done her so dirty. She'd been caught up in a time of romance that was deception. And since they'd won the championship and he'd gotten his medal, he'd dropped her for his real love and walked away.

She hadn't danced since he'd done that. And now she'd danced with Caleb and enjoyed it. The truth was, she would love to get out there and dance with him some more. It was fun, it was exercise, and it helped keep her mood up. But as wonderful as it had been, she was not over her dance partner using her love for dancing to take advantage of her.

She stood up, carried her empty coffee cup into the house, and set it on the counter. She was over it. She had to start living her life again but dancing wasn't something that gave her joy anymore; she just—*liar*. Okay, yes, dancing with Caleb had given her joy for the first time in such a long time. But no more. She wasn't setting herself up for messing her life up again.

She went into her bedroom, opened her drawer, and pulled out a pair of denim shorts. She put them on and pulled out a red T-shirt. Then she carried her tennis shoes into the living room, sat down on the couch, and put her feet in the shoes. She looked up at the photo of Niagara Falls that reminded her that she'd fallen over the falls, and wasn't doing it again.

It was time to hike. She needed to get out there, have some fun, get some exercise and not think about last night. She was not going back to getting her exercise through her love of competitive dancing. She had loved it and it had ruined her life—but she was going to move forward. She grabbed a bottle of water and her phone; she walked out the door, then opened the gate leading from where she was to the big pasture. This was good.

She walked toward the woods, careful through the tall grass and weeds, and found where trucks had made a tire trail. She enjoyed the walk. Just being outdoors had always thrilled her. She finally reached the trees and walked beneath the first large oak tree. To her excitement, she heard the trickle of a stream. It was a soft sound but it called to her, so she made her way down the trail that she decided was probably made from cattle that were put in the pasture sometimes.

Yes, since she had been living in the cabin, they had let the cattle come into this pasture and graze, so that's why the grass hadn't been terribly high. The cowboys had come through a few times on their horses as they herded them into another one, and that included Caleb. Two of those times had been on Sunday afternoons, and she had been home to see them on the trail. Now she followed the trail and made her way down to the small stream.

It was beautiful as it flowed along the rocky section, and the soft sound of the water was soothing. There was a large flat rock, so she sat down on it, so happy knowing this was here. Peace filled her as she listened to the soft gurgle of water and the birds singing. Maybe here she could find some peace for the day, and if she decided she wanted to explore more, she would. But right now, this was perfect.

She'd been there for about an hour, thinking over her life, her mistakes, and a need so strong to move forward. The fact was, if she didn't confront her pain, this would be her life: always alone. Hiding from a mistake.

A sound drew her attention, and she looked across the stream. There, standing on a hill on a fallen tree, stood a billy goat.

A *big* billy goat. He had a long, hairy beard and thick billy goat horns that he cocked to the side as he stood there looking at her like he was a sergeant about to command an army.

Then he let out a hard and loud *MAA-MAA!*

She jumped—the sound was so loud and shocking—harsh…demanding.

She wasn't sure what to call it.

What she was sure of was that it made her skin tremble and set her hair nearly standing on end as she stared, frozen in place, eyes locked with the demanding goat—

Then, to her startled surprise, he *charged* down the hill straight for her.

CHAPTER FIVE

Heart thundering, Jasmine stared as the billy goat slammed on his brakes at the stream's edge. She was now half sitting, about to jump up if it charged across the stream. But no, it pranced—*pranced* along the stream across from her. Then he lifted its head and bellowed again before charging back up to where it had been standing moments ago.

Breathing hard, she stared, shocked, startled, watching it jog out of sight—only to return instantly to glare down at her as if she wasn't getting his message.

Again, it charged hard and fast back down the incline, bellowing like the world was on fire as it came to a halt; yanked its head up and glared at her with fierce, demanding eyes.

She was nearly gasping, still in her odd sitting—

half standing position. What was wrong with this fellow—yes, it was clearly a male goat running on a rampage. As he raced up and then down a third time, her own brain screamed at her—*he's asking for help.*

Help.

Yes! He was calling her, wanting her to see something at the top of that hill. At least, if it had been a person, that would be her thoughts.

This goat, this large old-looking fella, was insistent. And Jasmine popped into a standing position, to which he bellowed even louder. She didn't hesitate after that, she stormed across the shallow creek bottom, not even worrying about trying to step on the stones. As Jasmine made it to the other side the goat charged up the hill and she followed. He glanced over his shoulder, then reached the top of the hill and spun to look down at her and he let out an excited bellow before he sprang back into action, racing out of sight.

Breathing hard, Jasmine made it to the top of the incline and saw him bounding through the, thankfully, low grass—the sunlight was less because of the trees, so the grass was short here. She followed, not too far away, and then she raced into mud. Only then did she notice that the goat had mud up to his knees. Ahead of her, she saw him halt knee-deep in the mud before letting out a humongous bellow.

He stood in a very large, round, mud hole that looked like a muddy pond… She gasped as she saw about six feet behind him a…a *head.*

A pony head—no, a donkey!

The poor gal, or fella, had only its head and partial shoulder still visible in the mud. And it wasn't moving. It wasn't moving or making a sound as it stared at her with huge, glistening, *pleading* eyes.

Her heart stopped. Her breath caught.

From the size of its head and shoulders, not much bigger than the goat's, it was clear this was either a miniature donkey or a baby, not more than about three feet tall, and very clearly in trouble.

The goat had stopped halfway between her and the donkey, and it stood ankle-high in the muddy water before the sand took over where the donkey was; Mr. Billy let out a thunderous bellow, clearly telling her to help.

Unmistakably he had come looking for help for his friend and now he stood glaring at her, demanding that she step up and do something.

What, oh what, was she supposed to do? Pull him out!

And then the donkey let out a soft cry—it sounded scared; it shifted its weight, then froze. Its dark eyes pulled her, and she slugged through the low water past the now unmoving goat.

What in the world was wrong? It was simply mud.

Then it bellowed lower, as if saying, "Go get my friend."

Then, on her next step, her feet sunk in the muddy sand. And by the time she reached the donkey, she was knee-high in the sand. The little fella or gal watched her, those dark-brown eyes pleading as it let out another soft cry.

And then the sand around her knees grew tight; she moved her leg and felt herself sink. She moved again and sank more; she pulled at her leg but it did not come up. Instead, it sank more. She then realized the donkey knew it was sinking, so she needed to get it out. She wrapped her arms around its neck, but when she pulled, she sank more in the sand.

What in the world was this?

She froze. *Did they have quicksand in Texas?*

She'd never, thank goodness, been in quicksand. But that was what this felt like, and she realized that the donkey knew it had reached a spot and was doomed if it moved. And the goat, oh the goat, had known it, too, and he was trying to help his friend by finding someone who could pull him or her out.

Was she right? Her mind raced as she carefully tried to take a step away to test getting the donkey out, but her feet did not move other than to sink. She stood still, her heart pounding as she once again tried to pull her foot free, tried to move something. But her knees were in the sand now and they weren't coming out.

Frantic, she pulled hard on the donkey but it squealed, loudly this time, and its sweet face turned grim. She realized the animal was sinking still. No, she realized she wasn't getting it out. And in that moment, she stumbled because she had been leaning hard toward the land, trying to pull it and when she did, she was now waist-deep and felt the muddy quicksand squeezing tightly around her waist.

The poor donkey still studied her, knowing exactly what she was feeling.

They were in trouble.

She reached for her phone. It was in her now muddy pocket but she pulled it out, lifted her muddy phone from the tightening sand. She shook it off, the sand squeezing around her body as the movements had her edging downward. Her legs felt as if they'd been squeezed into too-small leggings. As she realized the movement was sinking her quickly now, up to her ribs, she halted. Obviously, the donkey had already figured this out. She felt the shift again, this time not because she moved; it was just because she was clearly in quicksand, and quicksand sucked everything under, given time.

The old goat let out a soft *maa*, and she looked at him. It was as if he was trying to push her to calm down. To think, and not just think about how ridiculous sinking in quicksand in Texas sounded. That was most definitely what it was. She remembered reading about it awhile back, that it could develop when certain factors came together. The article she had read had been about a young teen hunting, and he had gotten caught in mud caused from underground water moving beneath dirt. It made the kid sink in quicksand and as she looked at the goat, she knew this was bad.

"Go home and get help," she called, having no idea whether that goat could help them now. She was on the backside of the Buckley Ranch where Genna had lived before marrying West, and unless there were cattle in the pastures, there weren't many who came out here.

However, she also knew they had amazing goats and one in particular was known as an old stubborn fella, that stood guard on the ranch. And suddenly she knew this had to be him.

This *had* to be Sergeant Two Toes, the most stubborn, protective goat around.

"Sergeant Two Toes," she said gently; his head immediately popped up high, and it bellowed, and her heart cheered, hallelujah! "Sergeant Two Toes, I'm trying but I need you to go get more help."

The words came out of a brain that was panicking

as she felt herself sinking ever so slowly—thank goodness when she didn't move, it took more time. It wasn't the sinking that now scared her but the tightness growing around her body. West was Genna's husband. He was the Buckley brother who loved the goats, who took care of them in honor of his grandmother. He was who this goat had to know. And this goat, though a long way from home, had to know his name.

"Go get West," she demanded.

The goat stared at her but then he lifted its head, his gray whiskers flopping as he spun in the shallow water, where he'd been smart enough to stop at—and then he raced toward the trees.

In her heart of hearts, she didn't know what was happening, didn't know whether the goat was going for help to the ranch or to see whether he could find someone accidently, like he had found her.

She didn't know but as she tried to move her legs, she felt herself sink again and she stilled, just like this little donkey had already figured out. The more you moved, the more you sank. And she knew in that moment that they were in trouble—big trouble.

In the article she had read, the young man who had gotten help while hunting had managed to call someone, and now she stared at her muddy phone and tapped it to make the call. But the phone was dead.

And if they didn't get help—the donkey had sunk more, the sand now close to its lips—that would be her, too. Or, from the feel of the squeezing and the no feeling in her legs, now a single thought gripped her: they could suffocate. And that might be the way it all ended.

* * *

Caleb had been bothered by last night at the dance and the way Jasmine had left. All night he thought about it and decided that this morning he needed to see her again. Needed to make sure she didn't think he'd meant anything by him wanting her to dance with him. It was just a dance. But obviously it meant more to her than to him. Something had happened in her life, he was fairly sure. And dancing meant something to her that he had a feeling wasn't good.

She rented the cabin that his sister-in-law Genna

had rented upon first coming to town. It was on the ranch, down on the road, with property from another ranch on the other side of the fence. But it was a nice piece of property, and the cabin had always been there. He hadn't been out here in a while—in the pasture, but not the cabin. As he approached, he saw the seating area outside the house with a cute set of colorful chairs. They were situated so that nothing was in your way of watching the sunrise or the sunset. He wondered what it would be like to sit out there with Jasmine and watch the sunset.

Not a thought he needed to be thinking about as he pulled into the drive and parked. He was getting out of the truck when he glimpsed movement across the pasture. He stared. In the distance, he spotted a goat blasting from the trees, racing in his direction. It was old Sergeant Two Toes, named after the fact that a goat had hooves but they were called toes, so Sergeant Two Toes fit because the goat always seemed to be in charge. However, it was unusual to see Sergeant Two Toes racing across a pasture.

What was going on? The old goat normally wanted

to watch all the goats play in the yard at his brother's place, which used to be his grandparents' place. The goat normally stood out in the pasture of his choice and watched whatever he wanted to, but charging across the pasture as if he were in a race to win was totally not normal.

Watching the charging goat, Caleb walked to the steps and knocked on the door. When he got no answer, he knocked again, and as he watched, the old goat bellowed. Goats didn't normally bellow, but that's what it sounded like as Sergeant Two Toes reached the fence. Instead of stopping, Caleb watched as the old goat took one powerful leap and jumped the fence, even at his age—wow, goats were amazing. Sergeant Two Toes landed and pretty much yelled as those toes of his touched ground and he finished his race, slamming to a halt in front of Caleb.

"What in the world is going on, Sergeant?" Something had to be, he thought, as Sergeant just threw his head back and let out another bellow, then he raced back toward the fence.

What? This was highly unusual.

As if impatient, Sergeant flung himself back around and glared at Caleb. Then the goat trotted over to him snapped at his shirt sleeve before he whirled away and raced back to the fence, jumped it again, he glared over his shoulder the moment he touched the ground. This time his bellow was so loud that it was clear something was definitely wrong.

No more hesitating, Caleb hurried to the fence, unlocked the gate, and pushed it open; then he jogged back to his truck and climbed inside. The tree line where Sergeant Two Toes had come from was a long way across that pasture so he drove, because this was not normal goat behavior. Something was definitely wrong because the moment he'd opened that gate, the old goat had charged for the tree line, no looking back as Caleb stomped on the gas.

CHAPTER SIX

Heart now pounding, Caleb followed. He reached the tree line the goat had already disappeared behind. Jumping from the truck, he ran to the tree line and spotted Sergeant waiting for him down the trail. So he jogged down the trail as Sergeant waited at the stream; Sergeant jumped the stream and headed up the other side. It was highly unusual for this goat that just enjoyed standing around on hills, so Caleb raced up the hill behind him. He reached the top of the ridge and saw Sergeant Two Toes standing in the distance at the edge of a muddy pond—and behind him, a woman. *Jasmine!*

And all he saw sticking above the muddy ground was her head and shoulders, and beside her was a donkey's head that she was holding up, so it could breathe. They were sinking in the sandpit that had obviously turned into quicksand.

"Help," she called.

He hadn't brought a rope; he hadn't come prepared. "Don't move in quicksand. You just have to be still. I'm going to get you, so hang on."

"Thanks, I figured that out. But this little fella came in before me and figured it out long before me. Moving is not something I should do. This cute little donkey had already shown me that when I came in. He wasn't moving, and thank goodness that smart goat knew what to do when I asked him to go for help."

"Yeah, Sergeant Two Toes is an amazing old fella." Caleb searched the area, then saw what he needed. "Hold on." He jogged over to one of the trees, reached up and grabbed a branch that was hanging, half broken. He twisted the limb and it broke off, so he yanked it down and then carried it over to the quicksand. Thankfully, it was long enough with spread-out, small limbs. "I'm going to lay this out there and what you need to try to do is get among those leaves, if you can lay forward or lay back. And if you can hang onto the donkey, do it. But, as much as I hate to say it, if you can't, you get out first and I'll go in for that donkey."

He held onto the end and gently laid it out; then, as it touched the quicksand, he moved it to her. Like the smart woman she was, she moved the branches so that she was as close to the main branch as she could get and then she looped an arm around it and looked at him.

"I'm hanging on but my legs…they aren't moving. They're stuck and being squeezed."

"Hang onto the limb. I've never done this but before I come in for you and then can't get you out, we're going to try this. From an article I remember reading, it's better if we're not both stuck in there. So lean on that limb and it'll help give you support so you can slowly work on one leg. Move it back and forth gently. I need to go find some more branches, so I'll be back." He spun away and back to the trees.

He needed backup. He pulled his phone from his pocket and dialed his brothers in a group call.

Ryder picked it up on the first ring. "Hey, what's up? You're doing a group call—something wrong?"

The group call was a signal when a cow was down and help was needed quickly. "Yeah, I'm here at the end of the ranch, back behind the cabin where Jasmine lives. Come quick, through the fence—it's open. Come where my truck is and come across the creek and up the hill—you'll see me. She's stuck in quicksand. Ryder, I'm trying to get her out but I need help. Bring one of those extendable ladders and you're going to need four-wheelers to get to us. Ropes. Strong, long ropes and um, water. They're going to need fresh water, Jasmine, Daisy Duke, and probably even the Sergeant. Whatever else you think of, bring it. I'll try to keep her up and hopefully out before y'all get here but she's into the shoulders and was trying to save that new small donkey. Thank goodness Sergeant Two Toes is the one who came and got me when I came here to see her."

"Gotcha. Hang in there. We're on our way. I'll make sure everyone knows."

"Thanks. Hurry." He hung up and stuffed the phone into the top pocket of his shirt—not his pants, just in case he needed it as close to him as he could get. He grabbed a thicker log that he'd seen and rolled it in that direction. It was heavy but it was round enough and long enough that he knew if he managed to get it where he wanted it at the edge of the water, that would be a good thing.

She didn't say anything; she just watched him as she held onto and leaned on the branch, concentrating as she tried to move a leg. Though she was hanging onto the limb, leaning forward onto it, she still had the donkey's head lifted up out of the sand with one hand.

He took his time to slowly roll the log in, watching how far he could roll it and still have it be steady. He had some help because obviously Sergeant Two Toes had done this before, and he walked in to where the sandy water was only halfway to his short knees. Good to know, he proceeded to get the log to where the goat stood; the log had the top area still visible. Caleb leaned on it and felt the solidness on the main end, but on the front end he felt it sink a smidge. He had a little levelness so he went back to the trees and he grabbed more limbs, longer and a little thicker branches.

He carried four of them in his arms back to Jasmine. There he laid them across the log and the tree limb that he had put out there, hoping he made something a little more steady. The tree hadn't sank much, so, to test it, he leaned on it and waited. Thank the good Lord it was in a fairly solid spot. He leaned harder on it, then held his hand out across the limbs. "Try to grab my hand. I have help on the way. If I get stuck getting you out, you stay out." Jasmine wasn't sure exactly what he meant, he could tell in her eyes.

"Don't come in here for me. I mean it. I'm the one who did this."

"I think you came in here to get that donkey. I think she's the one that went in there. Keep working your legs and give me your free hand." He talked, hoping he could get her mind off doing what he told her to do as she looked at him. *Gosh, she had beautiful eyes.* When she reached for him, he took a step into the sand and felt his first foot go in, so he grabbed her hand. Then, keeping the branches between them, he tugged her.

She barely moved.

* * *

Jasmine was tired as Caleb held tight to her hand. Her leg, the one she had been trying to move, was at least semi-loose now. She tried wiggling her right leg and couldn't, but she managed to start wiggling her foot. Little by little, she had it moving and she felt it kind of rising. When Caleb came back with more wood and he'd laid it across the mud—the quicksand—it didn't sink fast; it reached a depth and stopped sinking, like she had done. She was down to her lower ribs but the poor donkey had only her head sticking up. If Jasmine wasn't holding her nose up, she wouldn't be breathing and as if she knew that, she kept her little eyes on Jasmine.

"I can't let go of this donkey's head. She's tired and if she can't hold it up, she'll lay it down and be gone."

Caleb held her hand from the side of her, where he'd laid the layer of limbs. She had watched him breaking limbs off; then he laid them out on the quicksand and now, still holding her hand, he laid down on top of the limbs spread between them.

"So, I know you're not going to let go of Daisy Duke. My brothers are on their way. I promise, if I can't get you out, they will. They'll bring ropes and whatever else they need. But listen to me. I read an article on this and it says don't lean forward, lean back—so that's why I've laid this wood where it is. I want you to keep your hand under Daisy's jaw. Hold onto her as you lean back onto the limbs. Let as much of your back as possible rest on this wood. We have to keep your front ribs as free as we can for your lungs."

"Daisy Duke," she said, softly, smiling when the little gal's ears twitched at her name. "Help is on the way." Feeling better at this information, she then did just what Caleb told her to do: she leaned her upper body back as much as possible onto the wood and for the first time in hours, she was able to relax for a moment. "Thank you. I am so tired."

Caleb rubbed his hand across her forehead, brushing hair out of the way as she gazed up toward the sky.

To her surprise, he leaned over her, looking into her eyes. The man had beautiful eyes, and she could tell he meant everything he was doing for her.

"I'm just glad I came to find you, to tell you I'm sorry about last night. I hope I didn't mess up. Can we be friends?"

Her heart thundered. "I think we can…no matter what happens, remember that we're friends." Despite her now more relaxed position, she was having trouble breathing. Still, she smiled at him; his eyes held hers but he didn't smile.

"You just hang in there—listen, hear that sound? The backup has arrived. My brothers—they're on their four-wheelers. They're bringing stuff to pull us out of here and get us where we need to go, so hang in there, babe."

She could hear them. Heard the motors of their four-wheelers as they obviously had parked trucks somewhere and unloaded the all-terrain vehicles, come through the water and up the hill. As the sounds grew louder, she was so very thankful as Ryder plowed toward them with Zack and then their cousin Hunter on a third four-wheeler.

"We're going to get you out of here now for certain," Caleb assured her. "They brought everything needed to dig you out."

"Wonderful," she said, her voice soft as she watched his family roar to a halt and jump from their rides. Three tall, serious-looking cowboys came to stand beside the pit. "Hi," she said. "Can you help this wonderful brother of yours get me and this cute Daisy Duke out of all this mess?"

The oldest, Ryder, met her gaze. "That's what we're here for, so you just hang on. We're glad you were able to call us, Caleb."

"Me too," Caleb said.

She heard relief in his words. He had worked so hard and had probably been feeling the pressure on his shoulders that alone he might not save her. And she knew that Daisy Duke was in very deep trouble, and he did, too.

Just like that, the Buckley men went into action. They had brought a folded metal, extendable ladder and they pulled from the back of one of the rides. It was only about four foot tall, but as she watched, it suddenly became three times longer as they pulled different levels out and it grew. Then, right there beside where her torso and her hips were still hidden in the ground, they laid it across the danger zone beside her. It reached from hard ground to hard ground with all the wet, swampy junk in between.

Caleb looked at her again. "I'm going to hang onto you, and they're going to dig around your legs one at a time from the ladder, which will hold them. We're going to get one leg free, then we'll get the other one free. And when it's free, I'm going to pull you out of here."

"That's exactly what we're going to do," Ryder agreed. "So come on, cowboys, let's do this." He knelt on his knees and then laid out on the ladder; it held him. Zack then handed him a long-handled shovel. He immediately started to dig while Hunter went to the other side of the ladder and did the same as his cousin. Then Zack handed him a shovel, too. Together, they dug on either side of her left leg, both being very careful around her as they worked. And Zack, the quietest of the Buckley brothers, brought more supplies from their rides and handed them whatever they asked for.

Ryder looked at her. "Beneath your foot, you'll feel the shovel, so when you feel it beneath your foot and I lean it away to give your foot a little room, pull up. Hunter will do the same, but you have to pull up little by little. This could take hours. Then again, it could go quickly. When you pull up, the ground beneath your foot will fill right back up, but your foot will be on its way to freedom. We'll keep doing that until you get that leg up on the ground and we'll start on the next leg. So hang on, here we go."

And so it began, little by little, doing just as he said. They helped her ease her right leg up gradually, one shovel at a time. It had been awhile and she smiled up at Caleb, who had slipped his hand beneath hers and was helping hold Daisy's head up out of the muck. She was too tired from struggling to keep the sweet donkey alive and thankful for his hand now cupping hers and giving strength where she needed it. Thankfully, the sweet donkey was no longer sinking but was probably feeling all the tightening pressure around its body that she was feeling.

Caleb lifted his free arm and took the bottle of water Zach handed him, and then he carefully gave her a much-needed drink. When she was finished he took a drink then handed the bottle back to Zack.

"You're doing good," Zack assured her with a gentle smile from up above her.

She smiled at him and then at Caleb just as her leg came free—finally. She gasped with joy as Zack grabbed a rope and handed one end of it to Hunter, who then slipped it beneath her knee then lifted her knee up off the ground. Zack then took both ends of the rope and moved around the edge so he could take the pressure of keeping the leg up out of the sandpit. She had no energy left in her leg—no feeling, either. But it was up and safe as Zack held on and the other two cowboys dug hard on the next leg.

Then, at last, her other leg was free.

Instantly, Ryder demanded, "Okay, guys, let's do this. Hunter, now that you have free hands take Daisy's head and hold it up. Jasmine, let it go; he'll take care of her while we get you out. Then we'll free the little gal you've worked so hard to save."

Relief surged through her as she did what Ryder asked and let Hunter take Daisy's jaw while Caleb slipped his hands beneath her shoulders as Zack pulled the right knee with the rope while Ryder held the other knee. On the count of three, they all started pulling together and she was free, at last.

A grinning Caleb pulled hard and fell backward, and she went with him.

Free! She was free as Caleb's arms slipped completely around her, and he kissed the back of her neck.

"You're safe, sweet lady."

If she could move her aching and numb body, she would have rolled over to face him and kissed him on the lips. She couldn't move but felt the slow tingle of life as blood slowly began waking up her sleeping body.

"Awesome," Hunter called. "Now let's get this little donkey out that Jasmine almost died trying to save."

Immediately, both Ryder and Zack smiled down at her, wrapped in Caleb's arms and then headed off to save her donkey.

Tears slipped from her eyes as Caleb shifted, gently lowering her to the ground as he moved from beneath her.

He sat up and smiled down at her with concern in his gaze. "You're safe now, but from what I read, your body is having to wake back up. The exertion and pressure of the squeezing quicksand will ease up, so just keep relaxing. They'll get Daisy, don't worry. And Sergeant Two Toes is still overseeing. That smart old goat knew when to go for help and when to stand back and let them do their work. Now he's back in, knee-deep, making sure Daisy gets free. That goat knows too much—he moves around this country, likes to hop every fence he can find, so he roams free. I think he's been here before, and he knew exactly how deep not to go so he wouldn't get stuck."

"I think you're absolutely right," she managed as she let her gaze meet the proud old goat. *Sergeant Two Toes—what an astounding animal.*

He and this wonderful man and the other three had come to her and Daisy's rescue. And her life had changed in the process.

CHAPTER SEVEN

Caleb helped Jasmine sit up as her breathing got better and she wanted to watch them rescue Daisy. "They'll get her out, so watch but concentrate on letting your blood get back into your legs."

Zack handed them a rope that he had fashioned into a harness to go around Daisy's neck and jaw so he could hold the donkey's head out of the quicksand. Hunter wasted no time after Jasmine was free to take his shovel and dig under the donkey's front legs first. Because the donkey's legs were smaller and thinner and not as deep, he had them each dug out fairly quickly, and Ryder slipped another rope beneath the little gal. As Hunter continued to dig like Superman, they had the little gal out far faster than they'd gotten Jasmine out.

Zack was the one who reached in and lifted Daisy

to the final safety, and the weary little donkey instantly hee-hawed, then collapsed as Zack set her on the ground. Her buddy Sergeant Two Toes charged forward and began licking her face and let out a loud *maa-maa*. Everyone grinned at the sight.

Ryder then carried Daisy to one of the four-wheelers and, not wanting to take a chance the donkey would get herself stuck in the sand again, he tied the rope still attached to her to his vehicle.

"They were so sweet to Daisy." Jasmine looked at him, tears in her eyes. "Thank you, thank all of you, for saving me and that sweet donkey," she called out as everyone came to stand around them. "That is one wonderful goat you've made completely happy."

And as if he knew they were praising him, Sergeant Two Toes lifted his head and bellowed with glee as his buddy, still lying on the ground, lifted her head and hee-hawed, her eyes glowing with joy.

The long braying had every one of them laughing in happiness and relief, and Caleb was so thankful for the way everything had turned out. If he hadn't come out today, this wouldn't be the celebration they would have been having.

His heart gripped tightly at the thought and smiled with all of his heart into the thankful eyes of Jasmine.

"Y'all take my ride back to your truck, and we'll follow after we have everything loaded," Hunter said.

"Thanks. Is that okay with you?" Caleb asked Jasmine, who was cuddled in his arms whether she wanted to be or not.

She took a deep breath and nodded. "Yes, that sounds fine."

"Thanks, little fella." He grinned at his young cousin.

Hunter grinned back. "I'm not that little. You're just a big fella."

"True, but I will say you and my brothers are awesome." He called another thank-you out to his brothers, and then he gently picked Jasmine up and carried her to their ride. "I have a feeling you're ready for a shower and some air conditioning."

"That sounds good," she said.

Her arms around his neck and her eyes on his all made his heart have palpitations he'd never felt before.

He settled her on the back of the ATV, then climbed

on in front of her in the driver's seat and looked over his shoulder at her. "Now you hang on, lay your head on my shoulder—I promise I won't think anything about it." He grinned, and she chuckled gently, showing how tired she was. Her eyes sparkled a little and that made him smile inside.

Then he turned back, turned the engine on, and she rested her face against his back. And it was as wonderful as he'd thought it would be.

* * *

Jasmine couldn't have had a more amazing rescuer. She felt his heart beating as she placed her cheek against his shoulder blade and closed her eyes. It could have been such a horrible day, but now it was perfect.

She slid her arms around his waist and held on. As he drove slowly, he drove with one hand and covered her clasped hands with his. Her heart had pounded from terror today, from worry for little Daisy, and now from happiness.

He put both hands on the handlebars and drove the

ATV carefully down the slope to the stream, then crossed it and drove them up the far side. She clung to him, so close she wouldn't fall off—she was not letting go. When he reached the top finally, he brought the ATV to a stop beside his truck on the passenger side; then, before she could get her leg off the four-wheeler, he scooped her into his arms and carefully placed her on the seat, mud and all.

"But, the mud," she gasped.

"It'll wash out. All I'm interested in right now is making you more comfortable. I was worried you were so tired you might fall off but you proved me wrong."

"Thanks so much. So what will happen to my two new buddies?"

"The guys will make sure to get them home. I'm sure that they'll carry the little donkey with one of them on the four-wheeler and then good ole Sergeant Two Toes will follow them—or, who knows, lead the way. But they'll get back to where they're going. Never fear about that Sergeant Two Toes. He roams freely, and I've got a feeling now that he knows you and that you rescued his little buddy, you might start seeing him. He might drop by from time to time. So just be ready—but no following him into the muddy waters anymore. I'm going to give you my number, and if you need anything, you call me. If I can't be here, one of my brothers or my two cousins will be. Agree?" He pulled to a halt in front of her cabin and turned to look at her.

She smiled, liking the protective tone in his voice and the look in his eyes. "Agreed. I'm feeling much better, and a hot shower will be wonderful. I bet you'll be glad to get in your own shower."

"Yes, I will. Do you need me to come in? Anything I can do to help you?"

Kiss me. "No, I…I'm good. But, thank you for coming to see me this morning."

He'd already opened his door and now he jogged around and open her door giving her a moment to push the kiss idea away.

"I came this morning to check on you and make sure you're okay after watching you drive away last night. I'm thankful I came."

She reached out and laid her hand on his sandy arm. "I'll owe you forever. And, honestly, if you ever need anything, just let me know, okay? Don't know if I can save you from something like quick sand, but if you need help with anything, I'd love to try—I need to pay you back somehow."

"I'm not expecting anything but a call if you need me again."

They just stared at each other, her heart on a rampage. "All right, the shower is calling my name. Then I'm probably going to sit down and just be thankful."

He smiled, took her hand and helped her from the truck seat. "You do that. And who knows—maybe one day I'll need you and I'll call on you for payback. But right now, let's get you up those steps and inside."

Still holding his hand she stood still, making sure she was steady so he wouldn't be worried. Then she let him lead her up the steps to her door. "I'm good. Now go home and get your shower and know you are greatly appreciated by me, and my two new buddies, Sergeant

Two Toes and Daisy Duke."

He grinned. Then, to her surprise, he lifted her hand to his lips and kissed her still sandy knuckles. "I'm glad I came and was here for you and them."

Her heart stilled as he'd kissed her hand and words froze as their gazes locked once more. "Me too," she managed, then opened her door and went inside. It was cleanup time, and get her head on straight time.

But even the shower didn't straighten out her thoughts. She felt better afterward but her thoughts were still crazy. She made herself a cup of coffee and walked outside to sit down in one of her chairs, her gaze facing the road, not the pasture where she had been earlier.

She had not been sitting there long, her mind whirling and her world tumbling around, when she saw Genna driving toward the house. Sweet Genna—of course all of her brothers-in-law and her cousin-in-law had come to her rescue, so she must have heard the news from them.

Genna pulled to a halt and then hurried from the car. "I am horrified to hear what happened to you," she said. "I'm so thankful that Caleb got to you and was able to call for help. How are you feeling?"

Jasmine waved at the chair for her to sit down. "I'm better. I'm alive, and I'm not hurting. Yes, I'm tired but you're right, thanks to Caleb and that goat—My goodness, I love your goat and your baby donkey. I'll have to come see them. But your family saved me, and I'm great."

Genna smiled a huge smile. "Wonderful. I came just as soon as I heard what happened. Caleb came by to check on Sergeant Two Toes and Daisy Duke. He said he did it because he knew you're going to be wondering about them. He hadn't even been home to wash the sandy mud off himself after dropping you off. I was already coming out the door to get in my car and come this way after Ryder brought my little donkey and her guardian Sergeant Two Toes home. He also had come to ask me to come check on you, so I made him happy. Do you need anything?"

He had wanted her checked on. She smiled, unable to stop herself. "No, I'm good. I'm just, uh, I…well, I'm troubled."

"About?"

"Caleb didn't hesitate, he went to work instantly, trying to figure out a way to save me. And yes, I assume that any man worth anything would have done the same thing. But he's the one who did it for me, and well, he came out because of last night. I wasn't really nice to him after dancing with him. I just walked off and…I need to apologize to him, maybe explain my weird reactions to dancing with him."

Genna's lips hitched upward. "Well then, I have exactly the place to do it. We're going to have dinner tonight, and I want you to come. You can meet all my goats and you can check up on Sergeant Two Toes and Daisy Duke. How does that sound?"

"You know, I haven't really done anything to get to know people on a personal basis. I know you because we work together."

Genna laughed. "Oh yes, I've definitely noticed that. But now it's time for you to start getting to know everybody else. It doesn't mean there's anything romantic or anything. Don't get that idea."

"Okay, you're right. It is time, so I will start trying to put myself outside my barriers."

Genna's gaze turned a little more serious. "Yeah, you have barriers. You put them up very carefully, and I'm not the only one who has noticed them. So don't worry about that. No pressure. But if you have anything that you need to talk to me about, I'm always here. I've had my own troubles. Not that I'm comparing them to yours, since I don't know what yours are, but something tells me you need to talk. Or maybe I'm not the one you need to talk to. Who knows—you may need to talk to, say, Caleb. I didn't talk much until I met and talked to West. He listened, and it was something that I needed to do, but you went through something with Caleb, so maybe he's the one you need to trust with your thoughts too. If you're going to start stepping out there, taking a little chance, maybe he's the one."

"I'm not going to push something I don't know if I'm ready for, and in all honesty, what happened to me doesn't really compare to what happened to some people. Stupidity is a very embarrassing thing and that's the way I look at my experience. Total and complete stupidity. And that's something that I can guarantee won't ever, *ever* happen again. I'm not that way, usually, but sometimes emotions can bring things out in you that you didn't realize you had, and for me it was getting too involved. It messes up my practicality, my clear-headedness, and I made the mistake of my life. Stupidity." She couldn't help it; she laughed. It was the first time she laughed about this idiotic thing she had done, and when she looked at Genna, she was smiling too.

"So, I'm getting from you that what you just said was a good thing, right?"

She grinned. "Yes, it was. I'm smiling about it. I can't tell you how that made me feel to be able to grin about something that really was a bunch of hogwash. So thanks for coming. I don't know, maybe getting trapped, knowing I could have died, maybe that helped me see clearer."

Genna reached out and laid her hand on her arm. "It

could have. I mean, sometimes we take things so seriously in our hearts, things we shouldn't, and it takes an almost life-and-death situation to wake us up, to show us there's more to life than constantly thinking about something we did that was stupid. I'm not saying what you did was stupid." She laughed, and so did Jasmine. "I'm just saying that maybe you should laugh and get over it and move forward. Moving forward is a great thing, I can tell you. I moved forward, and it has made my life wonderful."

Jasmine took a deep breath, stared at her friend, and then nodded. "Me coming here was a huge step, really huge step, and when my mom came here and visited, she was so determined that I come here. Maybe that was because she felt it was the right place. I'm glad I came, I'm glad I know you, and I'm so glad you came out to see me today. And yes, dinner tonight will make much more of a great ending to a traumatic day, so what time?"

Genna leaned forward and hugged her. And then gave her directions out to her part of the ranch. She told her to come prepared to meet a bunch of fun, happy goats that would love to play with her, and the little donkey that hadn't lived there long who didn't like enclosures and had met her today. And the grandpa to all of them, Sergeant Two Toes, who had been looking out for Daisy Duke and for Jasmine.

And so, after a few moments and talking a little bit more, Genna got in her car and headed out, and Jasmine continued to sit in her chair, feeling much better about the day.

Maybe it was her first step in a new direction. She was good with that; she just had to take it one step at a time. But maybe this time in a different direction.

CHAPTER EIGHT

Jasmine felt better by the time she headed toward dinner at Genna's place. And though she wanted to get a little bit nervous about going out to the house, she wouldn't let herself. She got in the car and here she was, driving down the little dirt road that led to what she knew was the oldest home on the humungous Buckley Ranch. This was the house that the Buckley brothers' grandmother and grandfather began their life in. Where they combined their lives: her family's love of raising goats and his family's love of raising cattle. And this was where they had kept it going all these years.

Jasmine had heard many stories about the cute goats and the donkeys that gave them something to play on.

The store had begun as an online store and then,

once Genna had moved to this cute little town and opened a real store, women flocked here to buy clothes and have their picture taken in Lone Star. Her mother had been one of them. Her mother, who had visited and told her: "You need to go there and start a new life. There are cowboys everywhere."

At that point, Jasmine couldn't have cared less about a cowboy after having gone through what she'd gone through. But she'd come here for that dance—a dance that started after her mother told Genna the town needed something like a dance to help bring her daughter to this town. And it was pretty hilarious to her that a dance was something to help her.

And she had come finally and had enjoyed watching everybody have a good time, not that she planned to join in, but the people were amazing and she knew this was where she would want to start over. So here she was, and now she was at the ranch. The big, huge, beautiful red barn stood out as she drove down the lane and there, standing at attention in front of the barn, was sweet Sergeant Two Toes.

Smiling as she brought the car to a stop, and as the

amazing goat's gaze landed on her, she opened the door and got out of the car. "Hello there, Sergeant Two Toes. I'm so glad to see you again."

She approached him as he strutted over to her, ducked his head, and nudged her hip with his horns carefully, so he didn't hurt her. Then he lifted his head and let out a bellow that was loud and happy, not the one that had sounded the alarm for sweet Daisy Duke. She busted into a smile and, unable to help herself, she reached out and embraced him around the neck.

He let her, snuggling in as she rubbed his back while hugging him. "Thank you, thank you, you big, sweet goat. You are not just a sergeant—you are a hero. My hero." She leaned back and the goat's big eyes dug into her; she leaned forward and he let her kiss the top of his nose—not his nose but the hair that led to it. She loved him, but she wasn't kissing his nose.

When she looked up, she was startled to see Caleb at the edge of the barn, hands on his lean hips, muscles bulging in his arms, and a smile on his so handsome face. She gave the cute goat a rub on the head and then let go of him; he backed up and snickered, as if telling her to go over there and talk to him. "It looks like he's telling me I need to say hello," she said.

"Well, we both know that is one smart feller right there. And I have to say, he is a true hero."

Her throat clogged. She nodded and then forced out, "Yes, my hero. Well, him and you." What else could she say? That was just the truth.

He strode toward her and startled her as he placed an arm around her shoulders and tugged her to his side and gently squeezed her shoulders. "I'm just glad that I was there. It was a hard and wonderful morning. All day, I thought about the fact that I was heading out to see you—I'm so thankful that I had you on my mind and could come help pull you to safety."

Unable to stop herself, she wrapped her arm that was next to him around his waist and squeezed tight as she looked up at him. *Oh, goodness why did she do that?* He was looking down at her, the brim of his hat bringing shade to his face against the sunlight behind him. In that moment, it was as if they were the only two people in the world. She felt a tear slip from her eye, he saw it and in that moment, he brought his free hand up and wiped it off as it rolled down her cheek.

"Don't cry. It's all good. Now, let's head in to see everyone. When I saw you drive up, I decided I better walk out here and say hello and hopefully warn you that they're all here. Genna decided it would be a good time for you to get to know the whole family a little better. They're all happy we saved you, and the ones who couldn't be there are glad that the others were. If you're not prepared, just get back in your car and drive across that bridge. Sergeant Two Toes may follow you, and then again, he may not. He's always on the lookout for trouble, and obviously that's why he followed little Daisy this morning and he ended up being the hero."

"In more ways than one."

He nodded. "Yes, you're right. So I'd say I'd race you, but I'm not going to race. I'll go around the corner of the barn; you drive across the cattle guard and I'll meet you there."

She had to force her hand to leave his waist, which was disturbing, but she ignored it. As he released his hand from her shoulder, she moved to her car and sank into her driver's seat. They chuckled because there, in her window, stood Sergeant Two Toes, and he had his face tucked in and he was grinning at her, his hairy beard almost in her face.

She wrapped her hand around it and smoothed the beard, then ran her fingers along his forehead between the horns. Her heart squeezed. "Okay, big fella, here we go. You might step back. I'll go slow but you'll have to give me space."

As if he understood completely, he stepped back and then she moved the car forward over the cattle guard and into an area that was on the side of the house where the other vehicles were all parked. She saw the gate and past the gate, she saw a whole lot of goats, big and tiny. An assortment of old and young. The moment she got out of her car, they charged toward the fence. On the deck of the house, she saw a whole herd of cowboys and three beautiful ladies, all chuckling as they watched her get greeted by the joyous *maa-maaing* crowd.

* * *

Caleb was in trouble.

Yep, he had been unable to stop himself from putting his arm around her, and when she had wrapped her arm around his waist and then squeezed in a caring way. He'd lost it. Yes sir, he was a goner, plain and simple, and he knew it.

He enjoyed dancing, enjoyed having a good time, but he had never, not once, thought past that before. He had watched his brothers fall in love, his cousin also, and it had happened unexpectedly. Still, *him*? He almost laughed, it was so far-fetched. But he didn't laugh; he held it in. He was the last one to ever think about getting married. Maybe one day but to think that, right now, standing here, watching this sweet, lovely lady simply walking from her car to a herd of goats would thrill him and have him thinking such a thing was never expected…

He'd stood there on her porch, not exactly sure why he was looking at the closed door between them, but it felt wrong after having pulled her from that sand pit. The back of his brain was saying figure out some way that he needed her just so he could have stayed and talked to her, some way to ask her for help like she'd offered. Instead, he'd gone back to his truck, his brain reminding him that he didn't need a woman.

He liked to dance with them but *need*? No, that wasn't something he had been thinking at this time in his life, so he walked to his truck and drove away. But Jasmine had been on his mind ever since. Now, he reminded himself that she was as against a relationship as he was. There was no way of not knowing that. She had looked up into his eyes, and he had seen shock like he had never seen before. But that shock had also told him that there was something there.

Those beautiful eyes had connected with his so deeply that it had reached down and jabbed him in the heart.

Jabbed—yep, that was the word. Now what did he do?

"Hey there! It's so wonderful to have you out here," Genna called as she came down the steps and followed the goats to the gate. She moved through them and then opened the gate, swooshing the goats back as she embraced Jasmine.

"I know I've invited you out before but you're

always busy, so we're glad that today, this amazing day of survival of my awesome friend, you said yes." She chuckled. "And that not only did Sergeant Two Toes and Caleb rescue you, they also rescued that cute little gal over there, Daisy Duke, whose determination to explore got interrupted today by sinking sand. But there is my sweet niece Hazel over there loving on her, or maybe telling her to behave and stop jumping the fence."

Sydney, Hazel's mom, came out through the goats. "Glad you came out, and yes, that child of mine was almost heartbroken that the new tiny donkey almost died today. But she's so thankful that you saved her—"

"Tried to save her." Jasmine smiled at Sydney. They were friends, and seeing that darling girl loving on Daisy made her so happy. "All the great Buckley cowboys saved me and Daisy."

"But you started it," Genna said.

Sydney agreed. "Yes, you did, and after we told Hazel what happened, she told us she would make sure that Daisy Duke would know that she's well-loved and maybe she wouldn't jump out the fence again to run out and explore. I didn't want to tell her that sometimes, just like Sergeant Two Toes over there, when they have that need to explore, you can't really stop it, so…" She paused as everyone who had gathered around chuckled, even the men.

The little goats were surrounding her. Some had lifted onto their back legs and propped their front feet on her thighs, and she rubbed their sweet heads, but concentrated on what Sydney was saying.

"We just need to warn you sometimes when they start exploring in one direction, they return, so to stop that, the guys already went out the back way so you didn't see them and put a square wired fence up around the quicksand area so you won't have to worry there might be more problems back there."

"That's great to know."

Genna rubbed the head of the little black-and-white goat that had its hooves on her leg. "They can only get through it by jumping really high, so don't worry about more animals sinking there. But if Daisy Duke manages to escape here again, she may come visit. And Sergeant Two Toes will follow because, obviously, he's looking out for her. You don't always realize that about him, but that's exactly what he does. Isn't that right?" She looked at the guys.

Her husband, West, who had moved to stand behind her, wrapped his arms around his wife and squeezed. "Sergeant Two Toes is our lookout. Sometimes you don't think he's doing anything but roaming the fields, standing alert out there like he doesn't like to be around people or other animals. But in reality, we've learned that he's on the lookout for problems. He has alerted us when a calf is in trouble, led us to them before, and, just like this morning, he led our brother to you, and we're very grateful. As you well imagine, we love Sergeant Two Toes, named after his feet." Everybody laughed and she did, too. "Those feet carry him everywhere and he rules the roost, so it's a great name for him."

Jasmine's heart swelled for this family and she looked over her shoulder to where Caleb stood by the gate, holding back and obviously giving his family time to welcome her.

She smiled at him and felt it all the way to her *ten* toes.

CHAPTER NINE

Caleb was glad that all of his family was welcoming her and distracting her and giving him a few moments to get his head back on straight. He wasn't going there, where it wanted to go now.

No, he was going to be himself, the guy who had thankfully saved this young woman, and the guy who might dance with her again at another dance—if she would. But that was it.

Jasmine spoke to everyone for a few minutes, then her gaze settled on the goats now roaming around her. He watched as she gently began petting their heads as they nudged her for attention. He smiled, seeing how she clearly enjoyed each moment.

The yard surrounding the farmhouse was huge, having been created by their grandparents for the goats.

It was now and always had been to give them room to play and romp between the house and the gigantic, old original red barn that it was connected to. The high fence that connected everything was meant to keep the goats in the area. But the fence didn't always keep them in its boundaries. Goats were climbers and jumpers and full of curiosity and sometimes found an escape. But the tiny, short donkey had gotten out and she wasn't a jumper. Daisy Duke was basically a three by three foot walking explorer.

He knew that as of now, West and Genna probably had already searched the yard, trying to figure out how the little donkey escaped. The two older, regular-sized donkeys never tried to escape, enjoying being part of the recreational entertainment for the goats. As he thought that, across the yard, two goats leapt onto the back of one donkey, and another goat jumped onto the back of the other donkey.

"Oh, look!" Jasmine gasped, and everyone smiled as they turned and saw what they expected: she'd seen for the first time what they were all accustomed to. Goats loved to leap and play on everything, and that included donkeys' backs.

"They like to play on donkeys," Caleb said.

"Yes," Genna added. "Watch how calm they are. The donkeys enjoy just standing around and letting the goats climb on their backs after they'd climbed on the playground that helped them learn to climb on other things. It's not mountains and rough terrain but it's exciting to them. They actually sometimes try knocking each other off these two older donkeys, but so far Daisy Duke hasn't been like that for them. She doesn't stay still long enough and she's barely off the ground. She was part of a program of animals that they take to visit hospitals but they decided not to use her because she is too inquisitive. She won't stay still long enough for the patients to pet her, and so we took her in. And obviously, she doesn't like enclosures. As you can tell watching her now, she's tired. Like you've been—are you still tired?"

"I'm better but still not moving with as much energy. So what you're saying is that the quiet little gal I'm seeing right now isn't how Daisy normally is?"

Genna laughed. "Nope, Daisy Duke can stir up everything when she decides to throw her head back and sound off as loud as she can. You want to see goats racing around squealing, you will when she makes her voice heard. And we're all in agreement that she now knows the reaction she'll get and does her noise making to be entertained. So, we may have to find her a new home."

Caleb glanced over at a smiling Jasmine as she watched his little niece Hazel and Daisy Duke coming their way. His heart pounded harder at the look in her eyes, watching that sweet, beautiful little girl and cute donkey as they began jogging across the pasture toward them.

"Hi." Hazel slid to a halt in front of them and beamed up at Jasmine. "I'm Hazel, and I've just got to thank you for saving this cute Daisy Duke. I love this adorable baby girl, and I promise she won't be getting into quicksand again. I'll try to teach her when I come over here to play with her to be careful. So, you don't have to go in and risk getting pulled under. My mama told me and my new daddy, too, it's dangerous. So, stay out of it. Put things in it if you have to but mostly go for help."

Everybody was grinning as the little girl told them how to rescue something and not get killed. It was a dangerous thing and even though it didn't seem like it could happen, it could. Quicksand wasn't just in places known for quicksand; no, it was in odd places that absorbed water from a river or where the water flowed from a river to a pond. For some reason, places soaked it up and if that water ran beneath that ground, making a sinkhole, it was dangerous.

"I'm so glad to meet you, and I'm so glad that I was there for Daisy. I can assure you, little darling, that I won't be going back in. I watched your uncle Caleb do the right thing by putting all those long, very sturdy limbs on that ground, making it to where there was something for me to grab onto. And if you went in, I would come in after you, but I would make sure I did what *he* did so I wouldn't get stuck trying to get you out like I did trying to get Daisy out. And like he did, I would call for help."

It was true. She had thought about it and would never get caught in a situation like that. But she could have maybe helped the donkey; the problem was, she hadn't realized what she was stepping in to. She should have, because that cute little donkey had stared up at her with the big old wide-tooth-filled smile that looked as if she were in danger, and that in itself should have told her to hold off.

Suddenly, it hit her hard that she had ignored that in a lot of situations in her life. She should have seen the warning signs before she'd let a dancer charm her into partnering with him. They'd been there; she'd gone in anyway and let her heart be torn up…in more ways than one. They'd become engaged and champions in the process, and she'd been sucked in deep…

This beautiful little girl, who had lost her father before they had moved to this town, had found a new father, one who could step in and love her, and also share with her the memories of her dad she'd lost. But then she'd accepted a new life and helped her mom do the same.

And now as Jasmine stooped down and looked at Hazel and then at Daisy, she wrapped an arm around the girl, and placed her hand on Daisy's forehead and rubbed her between the ears. To that, Daisy let out a hee-haw like she'd been unable to do while in that mud. This smart donkey had known she was in too deep, but a little too late if Jasmine hadn't gotten there because of Sergeant Two Toes.

Jasmine had forewarnings in her relationship but had gotten in too deep.

"Hazel, I learned a lesson today. I learned that sometimes instead of fighting and roaming and struggling, that walking away is better than getting in too deep. You've added to my wonderful day."

And then Hazel wrapped her arms around her and hugged her tight.

"I lost my daddy, and I love him, and I know that he wants me to help everybody else get through bad things. I might be a little girl but I'm learning and I don't know what you went through but you're learning too." She reached out and wrapped her free arm around Daisy Duke. The donkey moved forward and rested her chin on Jasmine's other shoulder as Hazel looked at her again.

"We are both so glad you're part of us now. Your mama stays at our inn, and I was playing with my goats one day and I heard her talking with her friends while they were sitting outside on the patio. She talked about being worried about you after that dancing man used you to win that championship and then he ran off after that other girl."

Jasmine's heart squeezed tight as Hazel squinted up at her mother. "I'm sorry I listened to their conversation, Mama, but I just couldn't help myself. They didn't know I was just around the corner."

"It's okay. You couldn't help that you were playing and overheard them."

Sydney held her arms out to her daughter, and Jasmine let her go and watched Hazel step into her mama's arms.

It touched Jasmine, watching the two. They had been through far worse than she had been through.

It slammed into her like a huge boulder rolling down a mountain: she had been used, so why had she let that take over her life when these two had lost a love, a man who had loved them deeply? They had loved him, and they had moved forward in their lives. They stepped out, bravely coming to this town and in doing so, had made friends with these wonderful people and opened that beautiful B&B out there that her mother and all of her friends would come to on the weekends when they held the dances. Sydney had done what her grandfather had hoped she would do when he had left her that large house after she lost her sweet husband and he'd given her a new start in this sweet little town.

And her mother had come to town through Genna's store, because she had fallen in love with Genna's online clothing, and now stayed at that bed-and-breakfast. Her mind whirled as she thought of it all. So, in all of that, here she was, surrounded by these wonderful people but still lost in her stupid, crazy past. Thinking about a man who had used her to win a competition.

She was over it. Done. If this child could let go of deep pain, then she could let go of her anger and step out of hiding with an open heart. Suddenly, as if her life had begun anew, the sun came out from behind a cloud. It had already been a beautiful day and now it shone down brightly. She smiled, hugged Daisy Duke, kissed her between the eyes, and then stood up as her gaze went to Caleb. He looked startled, seeing her smile— probably didn't know what he was seeing but she hoped he could see she was free. *Free.*

* * *

Caleb knew something in Jasmine's mind had processed things around her. He'd seen her eyes working; he'd seen those beautiful eyes of hers glisten with what he thought were tears. But then, like the sun had come out behind them, her eyes sparkled. And when she had hugged that donkey and then stood and met his gaze, he had a feeling she had just gone through something, and he wanted to know what it was.

But he kept his mouth shut.

As if on target, his brother thankfully stepped in, grinning. "Okay, everybody, it's great to have you here. Now let's go in and eat. We'll leave all these animals out here to play like they love to do, but I'm ready to eat. How about y'all?" Everybody agreed, and he led the way.

Caleb, unable to help himself, placed his hand at the

back of Jasmine's lower back and escorted her up the steps and through the door that his brother held open for him and met his gaze. Oh yeah, West knew that Caleb was experiencing something he had never experienced before in his life, and he knew now what his brothers, who had fallen in love in the last little while, had experienced… He, the Happy Dancin' Cowboy, happy-go-lucky, no-attachments cowboy who loved his work, who had no intentions of getting tied down, had suddenly realized that sometimes someone steps into your life and everything else disappears.

"This picture here," Caleb said, after they had moved inside the house and through the next room into the dining area, where the large picture of all their family was, "that's all of us when we were younger. That's my grandad over there. Those two are my aunt and uncle, Ace and Hunter's mom and dad. And those little dudes are standing there in front of them. They lost their parents early on and they're basically our brothers now—we claimed them. And those surrounded by me and my brothers are our parents, who I think you've met at a dance on one of the few visits to town they've made." He grinned. "They come for special occasions but they travel a lot now, and me and my brothers and cousins take care of the ranch."

Her eyes were brighter, seemed clearer than before as she looked at him with almost what…*speculation?*

"I like your animals and your wonderful family. I met your parents at Genna and West's wedding." She smiled. "You have your dad's smile."

His smile spread slow and hitched upward on his right side. "Yup, as crooked as they come."

"In looks only, not in heart," she said, and shock waves of glee ricocheted through him.

"Next time they're in town, I'll make sure you're invited out to the ranch for a family night."

West walked up and slapped a hand on his shoulder. "Yeah, so welcome to the family." He grinned, looking from Jasmine to Caleb. "Is there something going on here that I need to know about? Wedding plans?"

He elbowed his brother in the ribs. "Hey dude, I'm just inviting her to dinner when Dad and Mom are home." The "gotcha" grin on his brother's face told him he knew exactly what he had done.

"I love your family," Jasmine said, laughter in the sound of her words. "I've just been kind of wandering on my own since before I moved here. But this morning, my trip to the quicksand was a wake-up call." She looked at the two of them. "In all honesty, I was in quicksand when I came here and actually being stuck in quicksand and realizing that there was a great possibility that I wasn't coming out of that alive, woke me up. So, I am very grateful, as odd as it sounds, for this morning. Out there with that sweet donkey Daisy Duke and that amazing Sergeant Two Toes, who recognized trouble when he saw it and galloped off for help, was a blessing and a wake-up call for me. So I'll just let y'all know, the quiet, keep-to-herself gal who y'all used to know is coming out of her hole. You may not even recognize me soon."

He was completely startled by her words and the way her eyes were dancing. And his insides were right on beat with her; just thinking about dancing with her sent tingles racing all through him. "So, I'm going to go ahead and lift my hand on the first dance at the next dance, which is, as of now, less than three weeks away."

West laughed. "Well, okay, let me just fill you two in. I'm glad that whatever you went through, you're stepping forward. That's always a wonderful thing and not always easy to do, so it's good that the quicksand woke you up. It's a great life out there, I can tell you— it's a really amazing life when you are open to changes and new people in your life and your heart. But not to get off into the deep end of the water, where I really don't know what's going on here," his look took them both in, "but you know our town isn't the only one that has a dance. There's lots of places where you can dance, so maybe my brother needs to take you for a dance. If you want that."

Her gaze had changed as her mouth closed in a suddenly thoughtful look. "You know, I'm not asking you to take me on a date, Caleb, but I think that might be a wonderful idea. As you figured out, I know how to dance but it's been a long time. Those two dances I shared with you—it had been awhile since I've done that, and it would be fun to relax and dance again."

Oh boy, he had to bite back a yelp of hoorah as he dipped his head and met her gaze full-on. "Well, I'll tell you what—let's plan on next Friday night. I'll make sure to take you to a nice place. But, you know, we're out in the boonies, so it's a little bit of a drive. If you're off work, I'll pick you up about six. That will give us an hour to drive, and we'll get there for dinner and dancing and then I'll bring you home before midnight." Man, he sounded like he was asking a high schooler out.

"Well, I think that sounds awesome."

Awesome. Her word ricocheted through his head. Yeah, it sounded awesome, and he had to get used to it. This was the first time he had actually asked a gal out in a very long time.

CHAPTER TEN

Jasmine noticed, after she and Caleb had set up their date for Friday night, that—it could have been her imagination—he had seemed a little more drawn back. Then again, that could have just been because his family was hilariously funny, and they came and sat out on the porch after dinner to watch the goats play. She went down the steps to sit beside Genna, and as they did, the goats came up to them—especially the baby goats. They romped and played, and then sweet Daisy Duke trotted to her, sat down on her rear beside where she was sitting on the porch, and, to her startled surprise, leaned her small donkey head against her shoulder.

"It looks like Daisy Duke loves you." Sydney looked at her with a grin. "The tiny little gal knows you saved her life. I have a feeling that she's going to be a loyal admirer of yours."

"True," Genna agreed. "She's not exactly like the other donkeys we have out here, you know. They're bigger and they love the goats jumping around on their backs. But she's not one to let them stand on her back, and they wouldn't be high off the ground anyway. You know I mentioned that I might need to find a new home for her."

Jasmine gasped. "Yes, but do you really mean that? That you might get rid of her?"

"Well, no, not like that. I would find her a good home. A place she would be safe and not find small places to get out of. We found a small place in the fence that she was able to push through and escape. She's done this a few times, and we just now found where she was getting through. She loves to wander around. Apparently, she likes to feel free and not caged in. She wants more space, even with a yard this big."

Jasmine reached out and rubbed her little friend's neck. Daisy instantly looked up at her and gave a little grin.

"When I drive through the countryside, I see

donkeys out in the big pastures, roaming around with all the cows. Can't she do that? I know she was coming toward my place today and just happened to get caught in that quicksand. But if there was a pasture that had no possibility of getting a spot like that, would that be possible?"

Sydney and Genna looked at each other and then smiled at her. "Yes, she could do that," Genna said. "But she's not the size of most donkeys, if you've noticed." She grinned. "She's a miniature. And the reason that donkeys are out there with cattle is they have a great roundhouse kick, and they actually protect the cattle and calves from wolves. They're like a karate expert—if the wrong thing comes around, they'll do a roundhouse kick and it will knock them out. But I don't think this little one will be able to do that and it worries me she could be attacked by the wolves herself. Also, there could be a mountain lion or bobcats. You don't see many of them, but Sydney here can tell you that they're out there."

"You're serious? I mean, I'd heard a little bit about the spotting of one and that helped you and Dustin get together with sweet little Hazel, right?"

Sydney smiled. "Yes. You know, you can have matchmakers—you can have a friend who sets you up on a date with someone they know, and it can sometimes turn out to be wonderful and it can sometimes be a disaster. But Dustin and I, our matchmaker was a mountain lion that was roaming my grandad's property when me and Hazel moved to town. That's how me and Dustin met. Not that it comes around anymore. But if you research them, they have a territory—it can be a large territory—and they one day will show back up as they roam the rest of their territory, so who knows? They can kill cattle, so I have a feeling that a little donkey running around out there on its lonesome, one as small and cute and nice as Daisy Duke, could be in trouble, so I'm more comfortable with her here in the fenced yard, just like Genna is."

Jasmine's head spun and heart raced. She and this little donkey were connected, and just the idea that she might be sent somewhere else didn't sit well with her. "Well, I live way out there in that little cabin, and I know you said you've thought about putting fences out there so you could put goats up around you, but then you ended up marrying West and now you don't need those fences or goats out there. And, Sydney, you have all those goats there for Hazel at your place—would a little donkey not be something good to have?"

"You're right. It might be a good place to have her but, as you can see, she doesn't like being closed in. I mean, you noticed when you got here and Hazel was over there playing with her, she was standing right near the fence. She walks the fence line, nudges it with her nose as if searching for a weak spot. We've all noticed it, and Hazel even worries about it. And, well, I don't know that she would be happy there at our place with so many people around and fences holding her in."

"So… but…" Her words fumbled because her head was telling her one thing and her heart was telling her another. Her head was screaming *Don't do it; you don't have a place for it; you can't keep her* and her heart was saying *Take her; build her a home.*

"Don't look so disturbed," Genna said. "I can assure you we're not going to do this without knowing where we're sending her and that it's a safe place."

"Okay. I know you wouldn't." She scratched Daisy Duke between the eyes, and looked at those big ole eyes that she had stared at as they were both stuck in that quicksand. All the donkey had above the quicksand was its eyes and its nose, and it kept its little mouth shut because it knew if it opened its mouth, the quicksand would go in. It relied on her fingers holding its nose up out of that quicksand as it stood still there, also realizing that if it kept moving, it would sink harder. And that did it.

Tears in her eyes, she looked at her friends. "I'll take her. I'll figure out a place. I'll find a place where I can put up a humungous, tall fence line…you know, one that holds deer in, one that keeps things out. I'll build a big one so it can roam and feel free and not closed in. And I'll get her some friends in there. I'll look and see what they like. I'll get Daisy some more miniature donkeys—that would be fun, if I got more little donkeys and they could play together like the goats do." The words rattled out but as she said them, she knew that's what she wanted to do, and she smiled big. "Honestly, y'all, I've never had a pet before and this little sweet gal is not my pet—she's my buddy. I'll buy her from you, but please don't send her away. I'll figure this out."

"Figure what out?"

They all looked up and there stood Caleb, his gaze locked on hers. She knew that he saw the tears but hoped he saw that they were not sad tears anymore; they were happy tears. She was getting a donkey.

"Well, Genna and Sydney were telling me that little Daisy Duke here doesn't fit in and that they're probably going to have to find her a new home. And unless they tell me no, I'm going to make her a home."

"Are you serious?"

"I am, yes. I helped save this little gal this morning but this little gal…well, y'all have no idea how much she helped me, the difference she made in my life. I don't want to lose her, and I have a feeling that if I could just build a huge fence, we could be happy."

She stared up at Caleb and then it hit her. "Do you think if I promise to rent that cabin for a while that maybe you could help put up a tall fence, one that would protect the little donkey from the mountain lions that might roam the country here on this huge ranch?" As she stared up at Caleb his smiled widened and filled her with joy.

"Darlin', I can do that. Yes, ma'am, I can."

* * *

Caleb almost did a somersault, something he saw Hazel doing quite often. The little tomboy tumble girl could somersault across the field with the goats, and it was fun to watch. Well, he almost tried to compete with her as he stared down into those amazing golden eyes. Building a fence, a tall fence, building it big enough to give that little donkey room to roam meant he would be out there closer to Jasmine, working and maybe hopefully spending time with her. And she smiled up at him as he had said those words that he would be glad to do it.

"Thank you. So what do y'all say?" She looked over at his two sisters-in-law.

They were both grinning. Their gazes went from him to her, and he knew what they were thinking. Thing was, he wasn't upset about it. He was thinking the same thing—that maybe the goats, maybe everything that was going on, was meant to be. Maybe he and this beautiful woman were meant to be.

"I'd say it's a done deal," Genna said.

Sydney nodded. "Oh yeah, I think it's going to be great. We built those fences that were just right for little goats, but I can tell you that I have a feeling that Caleb there—him and his brothers have built *many* fences, so he'll know how to build a fence to keep that cute little donkey in. And I like your idea. This ranch has goats and donkeys that come from our guys' history—their grandma loved them, and I can almost bet she would love that little one right there with its head leaning against your shoulder. It looks at you with those eyes like it's looking at its momma. So this is exciting—not only will this ranch have cattle and horses and goats and donkeys that like to play with them, if what you say is true, it might have a new fun herd of miniature donkeys that have plenty of room to roam if Caleb gets his mind on it and hauls in the work to do it."

Caleb saw the twinkle in her eyes and knew she was egging him on. He had a feeling that everyone could see that something inside him had changed. The guy who liked to dance with every girl around and not go steady with anybody had his eyes on one gal now. And if it took miniature donkeys to get him closer to her, that's what he would do. "Well, when we go dancing Friday, we'll talk about it."

"You're going dancing? You're going dancing, like, somewhere else?" Genna grinned, looking from one to the other.

Jasmine looked a little startled. Obviously he had spoken a little too soon. "Well, I told her we would go dancing Friday night if she wanted to, and she said she would."

"And yes, I will." Jasmine's golden eyes sparkled.

Where he had once seen her push away, he now saw something that had his heart raging.

"Well then—" He almost said *darlin'*. He had said it earlier without thinking, but he decided he shouldn't be pushing anything, so he held back. "That's what we'll do. We'll go dancing; we'll have dinner and talk about building a new place for miniature donkeys. I kind of like the idea. I have a feeling we might end up having a problem because as you can see, over there, Sergeant Two Toes is standing by the fence, observing all that's going on over here, and for him that's kind of unusual. He doesn't normally come around the fences that much. But like I said, he likes that little donkey. I think he feels protective of it, so you might have a visitor every once in a while over there."

Her smile widened. "And, as you know, that would make my day."

And she made his day. He hoped she would eventually turn his future into what he now had his sights on—wanting her in his life. He was in love, and the reality was he barely knew her.

* * *

Caleb had insisted on following her home, making sure she was safe and Jasmine had let him, unable to deny herself a few more minutes with him. .

"Genna beat me to asking you, but I'm really glad you came. My family enjoyed getting to know you more and I think you liked seeing the goats and especially seeing Daisy Duke looking better."

Now, he'd strode to her door and pulled it open and she wanted him to pull her into his arms. She found no words to reply to him as her gaze met his and tension roared to life between them.

Was he going to kiss her?

Her heart thundered as she slid out of her car, holding his hand with his words hanging between them.

"I enjoyed it so much. And I'm thrilled about Daisy Duke coming to live here. I can't wait to see that sweet donkey and maybe some goats romping and playing out here. I loved your family and everything they've done. Tonight… well, I know them and have been around them, but tonight was different. Caleb, you *saved* my life, along with help from your brothers and your cousin. And y'all not only rescued me but *my* soon-to-be little donkey."

He grinned widely, his eyes shimmering in the moonlight. "I'll always be privileged to have been the one who reached you first and who held you when you came out."

Her heart trembled at his words, and her breath

grew shallow. "Me…too," she managed, wishing, oh so wishing that he would reach for her and kiss her with as much energy as was radiating through her at that moment.

Who was this woman? This woman who had been hiding, angry, and never going to fall for a man again?

"Do you want to sit down for a little while?" she asked. They stood near her outside sitting area. She imagined in that second sitting there in the moonlight…and that kiss. Just the thought sent sparks igniting through her—it had been a very long time since she had kissed anyone, and that was someone she didn't want to remember…she wanted to wipe their memory from her thoughts and feel Caleb's lips— *Okay, back off, Jasmine!*

Caleb's lips hitched upward. "I was hoping you would ask me to sit in those colorful little chairs. I'd like watching the moon rise out there with you."

His words trickled through her with tempting thrills, and the sparkle in his eyes that she saw from the porch light tickled her too. She should have been worried but she wasn't. She wasn't afraid of him at all.

She… "I need to talk to you." And that was true. So true.

"Okay. But you sound kind of serious. Is something wrong?"

"No, nothing's wrong. I just feel like maybe I need to tell you about my past—why I don't dance or date. You've been so patient and kind and well, I just don't want you thinking anything weird about me."

He had walked over to the chairs and he picked the red one to sit down in. Maybe he was trying to make sure she knew he was going to stick around, and his actions told her exactly that.

She sat down in the yellow one. Her heart pattered hard. This time, it had nothing to do with the fact that she wanted to kiss him. It had to do with what she was going to say. "Okay, so I told you that I had danced, and that I had a dance partner and we competed. Come to find out, he just danced with me because he knew I was good and he wanted to win, and we did. And then, with that award and his name, he went with his girlfriend and told me goodbye. Here I thought that I had loved him, thought that he loved me. And all that time, it was just a game of deception. He used me, and like a woman with a wounded heart, I let it drive me to sticking to myself, staying away and not getting out on that dance floor again until…"

She toyed with the arm of the chair, took a deep breath, and looked at him. "Until, I watched you dance. Watched you have a great time like I used to have, and I watched every woman you asked to dance with you enthusiastically say yes." A smile came to her lips. "I didn't think bad of you. I thought you were pretty cool that you were so nice to ask everyone, and yet you never danced with anyone more than a few times at each dance. Yes, I noticed. Why is that? I would ask that question, but I kind of feel like it's probably for the same reason that I don't dance at all. Did you get jilted and now you're not looking for that to happen again?"

CHAPTER ELEVEN

Why had she asked him that?

Jasmine could have kicked herself as he held her gaze.

"You want to know why I don't dance with any woman much?" His gaze sparkled as his eyes held hers.

Why had she asked him such a personal question? He didn't answer as they sat there. It might have just been he was shocked that she was asking him a question considering she barely talked to him before the accident he had rescued her from. That echoed through her mind: *Was that part of why she was drawn to this guy—because he had rescued her?*

She pushed it out of her head. No, he was a nice guy and he had not done anything to make her mad, so she needed to walk back a little bit.

More than a little bit. "Maybe I was being intrusive…I shouldn't have asked that question. Listen, I really enjoyed being at your family's home tonight and meeting all the little goats and donkeys. I can't wait for you to come get my fence done. Are you sure you want to do that?"

Oh, she had jabbered far too much.

He hitched his lip up on one side. "Okay, well, I do want to help with the fence and getting it ready for your little donkey. And I wasn't mad for you asking why I dance so much but don't repeat my dance partners a lot. I'm glad you're curious."

"Okay, I shouldn't have asked that. You can dance any way you like, it's none of my business."

"I didn't say that. I'm curious about you too."

"Me asking the question makes me intruding into your privacy. Sorry about that."

"It's fine." He chuckled. "You get riled up really easy, Jasmine. I'm just not the kind of guy who's going to dance with the same person over and over again and give them the idea that there's anything between us. I'm not ready to settle down like my brothers have been."

He needed to correct his statement, not that he was sure that he was thinking straight. He wasn't just going to jump on the boat if he wasn't ready to get married or anything. My goodness, they had only danced twice together and gone to his brother's and his grandparents' home. His brain was kind of sliding over to the side a little bit; he needed to get it straight. "I'm just not the kind of guy who's going to lead somebody on by dancing with them a lot unless they're the kind of gal I know is doing it for the same reason I'm doing it—to have a good time."

She picked at the arm of the chair again. He hadn't asked her anything private; he hadn't done anything but asked her to go to a dance with him and rescued her from dying, so why was she acting so strange? She stared into those gorgeous eyes of his, and there was the answer again. As much as she didn't want to be attracted to anybody, she was and had been, and then he had rescued her.

"Okay, well, I guess I need to go in. I need to go to bed and, um, I'll probably see you sometime this week before we go out on Friday, right? I mean, why did I say that? I'll just see you on Friday." She stood up, feeling completely like she was walking off a ledge and he was laughing internally about the clumsiness in her words. She might be a great dancer, graceful and on target and on rhythm, but when she got nervous, her brain went elsewhere and her words came out confused, and obviously it made him smile. He was still sitting in his chair but he was beaming up at her with that gorgeous smile of his. "I didn't mean to say anything to make you feel uncomfortable."

He stood up. He looked as though he started to reach for a strand of hair on her shoulder; then he pulled his hand back and stuffed it in his pocket. "You don't have to be nervous around me. But if you can't help it, then I guess that's a plus. I mean, unless you're nervous because you're scared of me but I didn't give you anything to think that."

She laughed; she couldn't help it. She sighed. "Okay, this is ridiculous. I don't normally talk a lot when I'm…okay, when I'm attracted to someone. There, it's out, and it will help me not be nervous anymore. I don't *want* to be attracted to you or anyone.

Just so you know. It's out there between us, but I am a loner. I used to love to dance and I've agreed to go dancing with you. In all honesty, I am kind of looking forward to it…but no ideas. I'll try to get my words straight now that it's out in the open and you know, I mumble jumble around all the time. Thank goodness it doesn't happen out on the dance floor. So when we go dancing, you can relax—I'll enjoy myself and I'll make sure you enjoy yourself. We will dance to hog heaven and back if you want to. I just can't guarantee that I'm not going to muddle things up with my words."

There. And now he knew she couldn't really talk very well when she was attracted to someone. That was probably one reason her dance partner had put up with her while they were dancing in competition—and why, the day he had put his arm around the other woman and had given her a kiss in front of Jasmine, then told Jasmine that *that* woman didn't stumble around on her words like an idiot when he was around.

Wow, those words still rang in her ears.

She still didn't understand why she did that; normally she was a calm, not overexcited person, and thankfully, since she had watched that dude walk away with his real girlfriend, she hadn't been attracted to anyone. Hadn't had to experience this mumble jumble going on inside her right now.

"I'll see you. Good night." And with that, she didn't look back; she just walked the few steps to her door, entered it, and locked the door behind her. She hoped—oh, how she hoped—that by the time she saw him next, she had her crazy insides and her blubbering words under control.

* * *

Caleb's mind buzzed like a swarm of wasp all the way to his house—she was attracted to him and he made her stumble on her words.

Jasmine had talked as if she were totally rattled. He hadn't ever been around her that much—well, really, to listen to her talk because when guys were around, she just didn't talk that much. But she'd said, *I don't want to be attracted to you or anyone.* But she'd added the anyone. And now he realized watching from a distance

151

he saw her having conversations and she never seemed rattled.

So what now, knowing he rattled her—that should be good, but she'd made it clear that it wasn't.

Did he want her to think that way? He hadn't wanted anyone feeling that way before, now he wondered about it as he went home to sleep—or try to sleep.

The next morning, that's what he did: he got up and he went to work. He pulled up to the ranch barn and saw his cousins' and his brothers' trucks all parked there. They were supposed to be herding cows today, which was a good thing. It meant he didn't necessarily have to talk that much and he hoped nobody asked questions, because he was tired of answering them. They had seen him last night; they had seen that he probably was attracted more than normal for him, and he expected to get drilled about it.

He sat in his truck with his hands on the steering wheel. He took a deep breath and thought about backing up and going to find something else to do because when they started asking, what was he going to say? *Oh, she quit talking to me last night and practically ran into her house?* No, she didn't slam the door but she had it closed firmly between them because she is attracted to me—nope, not going there.

He got out and walked into the barn, prepared to get interrogated by them all, but determined to hold back the information plaguing him.

They stood around the coffee table, all dressed in their boots and their jeans, with their gloves stuck in their pockets. They were all ready to go work some cattle. Basically, they had to herd them to a certain area and then it was time to doctor the animals and because he saw the branding iron, they were obviously going to brand some, which was good. Again, it meant less time to talk.

Ryder held him out a cup of coffee. "Well, we thought you might beat us here. Then again, when you didn't, we thought you might not come at all. You sure did look happy last night."

He took the coffee and stared at his brother. "So can I not have a good time?"

He glanced around. Everybody was grinning.

Ryder's grin got bigger. "Oh, you can have as much fun as you want. We're just kind of excited."

"Okay, whoa, Ryder. You're getting a little ahead of yourself here. I danced with her and she came to Genna and West's and—"

"You rescued her from a load of quicksand." Ace grinned.

"Me rescuing her from a load of quicksand doesn't mean anything. I would have done that for anybody." Yes, he would have, but they didn't need to know that he really wanted to rescue her. He about had a heart attack when he saw the problem.

"Yeah, that's true," Ryder said. "But that look you were giving her last night at dinner—well, that kind of told the story."

All of them were grinning now.

He held up his hand. "Okay, fellas, come on, don't go giving me a hard time. She's not interested."

West cocked his head to the side. "Well, she might not have known it but we saw her give you a couple looks too. We all talked about it already and we all saw it, so I'm not crazy."

He looked away and gritted his teeth. He needed to keep calm. He looked back at him. "Y'all know I just like to dance." He stumbled on words. They knew he didn't date much; they knew he wasn't the only one in the group who had been dropped early on and hadn't come out liking it, so he was the one who didn't get serious. Besides that, he had time.

He didn't tell them what they wanted to hear, which was that, yes, this was different with Jasmine. Just the sound of her name had a different ring to it. *Jasmine*. It was beautiful, like her. He realized his thoughts had probably shown on his face as all of his brothers and two cousins were now grinning in a huge way.

"Come on, quit that. We've got work to do. I'm getting on my horse."

With that, he finished his coffee and set his cup down, then he turned and walked out of the barn and headed toward the other barn where the horses were. This was done for today; they had pushed him and one thing about him—he didn't like being pushed by anybody, especially if they were having fun doing it. He rolled his eyes as he entered the second barn, walked to the back, and started settling his horse, Lightning. "Yeah, we're going riding today. And if they get to bugging me, we're going to ride fast and hard. How's that sound?"

Lightning let out a whinny, lifted his head high, and flagged its tail so hard that it slapped him in the back.

He laughed. "Yeah, I totally agree. I'm glad we're on the same page."

CHAPTER TWELVE

It was a beautiful day as Jasmine drove into town. She had slept well after a lot of tossing and turning when she first climbed into bed. Then she had focused on the fact that she was going dancing Friday night, no strings attached, and she was going to enjoy it. And then she had slept.

Yes, she loved to dance. She probably loved to dance more than the dancing cowboy who was taking her. Everybody would probably be talking but she had forced it into her brain last night as she laid there, looking up at the ceiling, that she couldn't control that. What she could control were her emotions and feelings and learning to enjoy dancing again, but this time without letting her heart get involved. That had been her downfall before.

Of course, there was that voice in the back of her head shouting, *But Caleb isn't the same as that jerk you gave your heart to before!* But she just turned down the volume on that and let it sit there.

Plus, all that aside, he was going to come out and help make a fence for Daisy and maybe ole Sergeant Two Toes would come to visit her, too. Just that thought alone made her happy, and she couldn't help but smile. As she got out of the car and walked inside the store, she was still grinning.

Genna was off today, spending time in her new home life, one of the reasons she had hired Jasmine. Genna could spend more time at home and with her online business while Jasmine ran the store. Of course, most weekends, when people were coming to town, Genna worked because if they were a lover of her original online store, they loved to travel to Lone Star and have their picture taken with her and placed on her website. On the page where she featured photos of her with her customers wearing an outfit they loved. It was a big draw because Genna's online store was a huge success. Therefore, considering most customers came in on Fridays or Saturdays, she worked. Most of them would find a place to stay at night and shop the next day then come to the dance that evening.

It caused Jasmine's brain to whirl, especially considering that's how she got here. Her mom was a huge shopper on the online store and had been one of the first customers to drive here to go to the actual store and have her picture taken with Genna. *And* to ask whether the town held any gatherings or dances—and that helped start the monthly dances, and here she stood.

Today, she stood in the store, smiling and thinking about the day she had yesterday that started off with disaster and ended with her thinking about her future. It was great, an awesome feeling.

She shook herself from her thoughts. She had plenty of things to do: she had new clothes to get out, and as always, she wanted to make sure that Genna was happy that she had hired her. So that's exactly what she did; she went to work. And then the door opened and in walked Josie Jane, and Ruby right behind her. Oh boy, so here it was. She knew without a doubt they were going to ask her questions. Those two loved it when they saw romance in the air—not that she understood why they thought they had seen romance. They hadn't said anything yet but she looked at their faces and she just knew. "Good morning, ladies," she said as calmly as she could.

Josie Jane grinned as she walked over to her and put her hands on her hips. "Good morning to you, too, girlfriend. We just wanted to come by and see how you're doing today."

Ruby chortled as she also pulled a blouse down off the rack and looked at it. "I love this. I'm going to have to try this on. But I also love that you went to dinner at Genna and West's home last night. I know they were all happy that you finally decided to mingle a little bit. You know, we all know that you don't really do that—you come to work, you go back home. You come to the dances and stand back here, well, there with Millie— speaking of Millie, there she is."

And sure enough, the door opened and in walked long, tall cowgirl Millie. Her red hair was pulled back in her usual ponytail, and she had her jeans tucked into black Western boots with shining stars glistening on the side. And they set off her red, white, and blue cowgirl shirt that said "I'm here," loud and clear.

Millie grinned. "We all decided we'd come to see you this morning. We kind of have an idea that there's a little something going on with you and sweet, Happy Dancin' Cowboy, Caleb."

Jasmine now knew who had given him the nickname, and she was right on target with that name. She fought back a smile and stared at the wonderful three ladies standing before her. *What was she going to do with this?* They had left her alone ever since she'd come to town. She had listened to Millie's love story when the two of them had been sitting with Sydney at Kelsy and Ace's wedding, and Jasmine had realized, like Sydney, that moving forward was a good thing. But though Sydney had married Dustin and had moved forward, Jasmine had only continued to think it over and done nothing more.

Now, looking at them, words weren't coming.

"Look, darlin', I came down because you know that you and I have a lot in common. I don't exactly know your story because you're a quiet one, but I've learned that when a lady comes and stands beside me at that table on dance night something is up. They've noticed I stand behind that table instead of getting out on that dance floor and dancin' the night away. It's like I'm the refuge. Me and my table are the barrier between us and everybody else.

Well, I don't know if you've noticed but since Kelsy and that adorable, handsome Ace got together, I've started getting out there with her grandad, Lumas. I would be flat-out lying if I didn't admit that I had been watching him from afar. But when that big man—in build and in heart—comes over and asks me to dance, well, I can't say no. Despite all my mourning of my sweet Hank, I'm back out there dancing again and enjoying myself.

"I'm not letting myself think about what I've lost. Because, you know, I lost everything in my heart when I lost my sweet love, my champion that night when he had ridden, as always, the rough and crazy champion bulls he was so well known for doing. Then it came and took him out of my life as he stood down there, smiling at the cheering crowd. I gave it all up because I just couldn't go back there. And that included getting out on a dance floor without him. But, I've started stepping out. Us three gals who care for you decided it was time to come talk to you. And then we'll all go to work. So are you mad at us?"

All three ladies were looking at her with love and concern, and her heart squeezed tight because she knew they loved her. She came to this town because of what Josie Jane, Ruby and Millie had all done after her mother had asked them to help her get out of the hole she had dug herself into.

"Y'all, I love you. And what y'all have done for this town and everybody, including my mom and her friends, is wonderful. She is happier knowing I'm starting over here. I know she helped start this monthly dance because she cared for me, thought this would be a wonderful place for me, and she was right." She paused and tears welled in her eyes. "Y'all are a big, big part of that. But, I can't promise anything more. My heart was hurt, yes, really bad—partly because I was a fool. I gave it to somebody who did not need it or want it. Someone who was using me to win…" She looked at all of them and their eyes were wide and finally she thought, *What the heck?* "He used me and my heart to win competitions in dancing."

"I knew it!" Josie Jane slapped her leg. "I knew it!"

Ruby spun around, the pretty blouse billowing out as she did it, and she stopped, grinning at her. "We knew you could dance. We saw you that night and just wondered why you hadn't been getting out there and this explains it all."

Millie's eyes danced. "I saw that night when you stepped out there on that dance floor, something was different. And you may be telling yourself that maybe it was the fact that you had finally decided to go dancing, but I'm just going to tell you, I've noticed where your eyes are a lot when you're not out there on that dance floor, when you're standing beside me. I can see the direction that your eyes are in, and I can also see who's always at the end of where those eyes are going. And from what I understand, you and him are going dancing Friday night."

Oh goodness, what was she supposed to do? "Yes, I told him I would because y'all, my heart got broken over dancing with the wrong guy. I was at the top of the world, and I plummeted immediately. He dropped me right after he picked the award up in his hands and walked off with the other girl, so now you know I haven't danced since but…" She looked at Millie; her husband had loved her, and died loving her. He hadn't been a no-good dude who'd gone as far as to get engaged to her in order to ensure that he could use her to win a championship dance tournament. It was ridiculous, and she felt dumb.

Millie was back out there on that dance floor and she was starting to let her heart work again. Jasmine blinked back tears and looked at the gentle smiles coming to Ruby and Josie Jane's faces, and the tender eyes of Millie.

Millie stepped forward and took her into a hug. "Don't rush yourself, darlin', but I'm here to tell you that sometimes it's good to push that door on your heart back open and take a dance step or two. If it's not the right step, you'll know. But if you don't at least give it a shot, you'll never know whether you missed a wonderful chance at a wonderful life—and yes, I said wonderful twice and a third time now. I'm just telling you I had a wonderful life and I know, now that I've given my heart time to adjust to it, and that sweet Lumas might just be the next step in my life. If I don't take a chance on it, I'll be wrong. So anyway." She leaned back and looked her in the eyes. "I just had to come tell you that, let you look into *my* heart. And now I'm going to go back to work."

She let Jasmine go, smiled gently as she turned, and walked out the door.

Josie Jane gave her a hug and followed.

Ruby did the same. "Have fun, darlin', have fun. Life is *wonderful* if you just, yes, keep your guard up a little bit, but don't slam the door and keep a chain on it. And that fella is a awesome guy. I didn't even know when I told him or challenged him to ask you to dance—yes, it was me, and he did what I asked him to and thankfully you accepted—but I had no idea that you watched him. Because you can dance just as good as him—it's amazing. Y'all should enter a competition."

"Oh no, no, no, I will never enter a competition again. But I will go dancing. So thanks for coming to talk to me, but now I've got to get back to work or I might cry." It was true, so true. She didn't want to start bawling in front of everybody. But something in her life had just changed. She wasn't sure what exactly but maybe—*maybe*—she could do like Millie and step out from behind that table, and give that change a little bit more of a chance.

* * *

Friday arrived, and Caleb drove up the road to Jasmine's cabin. His heart was thundering just a little. It was an unusual feeling for him. Oh yeah, when he had been younger, just the thought of dating had given him a thrill but then he had adjusted to it and the fun of going out on a date was what it was. It was fun; it was just the idea of going dancing and spending time out there spinning girls around on that dance floor and watching them laugh and smile. He enjoyed it but having a reaction like what he was having right now as he saw the cabin appear? This was different—*far different*—from anything he had ever felt.

Yeah, he had listened to his brother West talk about Genna, and Ace, his little cousin, talk about Kelsy. And his friend Jace Calhoun, who had fallen in love with Lila, and then his brother Dustin and sweet Sydney and that little ole darling who they all called their niece now, Hazel. He was now among them. If this wasn't love, then it was a crush like nothing he had ever experienced before.

He pulled in the drive and parked the truck, turned it off and there, sitting in the red metal lawn chair, was Jasmine. *Whoa—* Oh yeah, he was in big trouble. She slowly stood, waiting for him.

He hadn't figured out how to make her happy, give her a great time and make her feel on top of the world so maybe, if he was lucky, she would feel an inkling of what he felt just looking at her. She wore those fancy boots of hers with the bottoms of a pair of faded jeans tucked into them, showing them off. But he didn't care about the boots. She wore a beautiful red blouse that shimmered, very similar to the one she wore at the dance that evening when he first danced with her. Her dark hair hung loose over her shoulders and as she stood there staring at him, she leaned her head slightly to the side and her hair dipped over her shoulder.

Dude, what are you doing? His heart pounded out in a frantic rampage against his chest.

He was taking this beautiful woman on a date.

Wow. Okay, get out of the truck, dude!

He opened the door, stepped out, and, then strode toward her. She hadn't moved; she just stood there, her hands on her hips as a welcoming smile spread across her beautiful face.

He halted in front of her. "Hi. You ready to go dancing?"

"Yes. I've actually been looking forward to it today. Thank you for asking me. This is, well…" She took a deep breath and sighed. "This is actually something that I need to do. I've always loved dancing and then my fiasco ruined that."

"I'm glad you want to go and that you're excited about it. And I promise you, we're going to have fun. It's a great place I'm taking you to. I used to go there a lot but then I got busy and we started having the dances in town, so I quit. But as far as I'm concerned, dancing with you once a month isn't enough." *Oh boy*. He had said a little more than he should have; he didn't want to run her off. But he meant every word.

"Well, thank you. I'll just tell you I used to love to dance and like you, once a month wouldn't have been enough. But I haven't danced in almost a year, other than when you took me on those two dances at the last gathering. So who knows? I might not let you get off the dance floor tonight."

A wide grin spread across his face in a flash. "All right, then. You ready to go? We better get this night started. No memories of before—just a good time and making a move toward future fun."

She held his gaze and those beautiful golden eyes of hers sparkled as she dipped to snatch up the tiny purse that she strapped across her shoulder and it hung on her hip.

"That's a giant purse you've got there," he said, grinning.

"It's perfect. It will stay with me all night and won't mess up my dancing. It's got everything I need—you know a little lip gloss to up my look." She chuckled and smacked her lips at him, showing her humor.

He liked this; he hadn't really realized she had a funny side to her. But he did know she had beautiful lips, and he did like the little bit of gloss on them. It wasn't as if she laid a lot of stuff on them, and all he could think about in that moment was kissing that little bit of gloss off them, then she could put more back on and he could kiss it off again. *Halt*—he had to get his head on straight; this was not where he needed to be going. Nope not at all.

He escorted her to the passenger side of his gigantic truck and he wished he had a small pickup truck so that he would have to sit real close to her in it. He held his hand out, and she placed hers in it. Instantly, electric lightning bolts flashed through him, as though he were exploding just at the simple touch of her hand.

She lifted her boot and put it on the running board that was a little higher than her knee. Then, holding the door and his hand, she lifted herself up and boosted herself into the seat.

He was tall enough that, even as high as the truck was, they were almost eye level; she was just a smidge taller than him sitting in that seat. His gaze dropped to those lips, then he yanked them back up to those beautiful eyes. It didn't matter whether it was lips or eyes; he was in trouble. "Alrighty then, let's get this party started."

He closed the door and jogged around the front of the truck, opened his—well, his door was still open; he'd never even shut it. He slid into the seat, practically just hopped up into the seat, closed his door, and plopped one hand on the steering wheel and the other on the gear shift. *This was happening.*

Heart pounding he looked at her. "I guess I shouldn't have said party. I should have said dancing, 'cause, darlin', tonight we're going to dance the night away."

He put the truck in gear, backed out, and off they went. He hadn't looked forward to something like this in…forever.

CHAPTER THIRTEEN

"Oh my word, I'm having a blast," Jasmine said as the country swing dance came to an end and she was clasped against Caleb after he had spun her around that dance floor and then pulled her against him when the song ended. She was breathless but managed to get the words out while looking up into his shining olive-green eyes that glowed in the light above the dance floor. The man could dance and he had helped her find the joy in the thing she had always loved and then walked away from because of her mess-up.

"Darlin', you are powerful on this dance floor. Man, what is that? Our fifth dance of the night? And you've danced amazingly, all of them so far."

She grinned at him, her hand in his beside her shoulder and her free hand resting on his chest. "I've enjoyed each one and I'm going to tell you—well, first I'll say I'm not interested in competing ever again. I just want to dance because I enjoy it. And if I'm dancing with somebody as good as you, it's unbelievable. I mean, really, not that I'm encouraging you to do so, but you're remarkable—honestly, you could win a championship if you were interested."

He laughed, lifted his head up, and then laughed at the ceiling. "That is a funny one. But I' m not interested in dancing for competition. I just enjoy it. It's kind of like, you know, when you're out herding cows—well, not that I know you do that, but if you ever want to, I'll sure take you—you're herding a cow, a whole bunch of them, and one of them escapes the group and charges, and you wonder *Why is he doing that?* I think it's because he sees that opening and just wants to feel free, and the cow or the calf charges off and then I have to go out and catch them. But I think they kind of get a thrill out of that, too. That's what dancing on the dance floor is to me—I'm a cow charging for the feeling of excitement that I get and enjoy. And honestly…"

A slow song started, and automatically, they began

two-stepping to the music without even going off the floor. "Honestly, I like helping people who aren't that great at dancing to get out on that floor and have a good time. When we started those monthly dances, I realized I was always looking for somebody who could dance the best. Like when I used to come *here*, usually late because of work. I'd get off and drive over here, and people like me, who really like to dance, would be ready to dance the night away. But then I realized at our town dance that I enjoy dancing with everyone—good, bad, and great." He chuckled as he gave her a spin before pulling her back into his arms.

"I love it," she said, meaning it with every ounce of happiness inside of her.

"I can tell. And since we've started the town dances, it's been great. And every once in a while someone comes to town who really knows what they're doing and I enjoy it. But I like taking the ones out who aren't sure-footed and encouraging them. Helping them, even if they don't realize that's what I'm doing as we take steps they've never done before. It's fun. But you…you have taught me a few steps in the same manner. You just lead the way and next thing I know, I'm doing it too."

It was the truth because as they danced, she'd slip in some steps she loved doing, though they weren't traditionally part of the dance. She'd added them in and Caleb picked up on them. Those steps would rapidly become part of the dance, and that was when her creative side took over. This simple two-step had quickly become more active, which was the fun part.

"You cowboy, are a pick-up artist. You've instantly adapted to every step I've thrown your way." He grinned and tugged her in and let her spin past him as he stepped aside but kept her fingers in his hand where they were supposed to be. "You can take on whatever I shoot at you." And that was what made him so awesome.

"Right back at you," he said, as she spun his way and he once again dipped her... She looked into his smiling eyes—her world spinning. They had danced five fun dances, this was their sixth. But above all that, right now, she was having to fight off the tingles and thrill of looking at him, his arm holding her up and wanting him to dip his head down and kiss her. Her heart thundered as he lifted her back to standing but kept his arm snuggled around her as their feet moved together. She could barely breathe, though she wasn't pressed hard against him, she was near. Just a slight move and they would be touching, but he didn't invade her space and she liked that about him; unlike some men, he didn't automatically pull her tightly close to him. No, he treated her like a lady.

But in her thought process, she had a sudden vision of what it would be like dancing with this man if they were a true couple, married... *Oh boy, she did not need to go there. Marriage? Why had that thought even come into her head?*

Another thing happened in that moment: she leaned her head against his shoulder while she was asking herself those questions. And in doing what she did, he instantly lowered his head against hers. That meant she was a little closer to his body.

"Are you okay? I really like holding you."

Her feet moved on their own as her head went elsewhere. Her thoughts became muddled at his nearness, at his breath touching her ear, of the sudden longing to look up into his eyes and kiss him.

"I'm good. I'm… Caleb, I've never danced with anyone better than you." It was all she could say. She didn't go into the fact that anybody being better than him meant nobody had been able to truly reach in and make her feel like she was the best. Not even the man she had won the championship with, who she had thought she loved. *Wow*. If she had, she had been an idiot then. Now she really thought she was, because she pulled her head back and looked up into Caleb's beautiful green eyes and knew without a doubt she had stepped across a line.

Dancing had a way of snarling up her insides. Dancing was what she loved. It wasn't the best dancers, who would have been what's-his-name, and now this Caleb who held her in his arms. It was the dancing…their wonderful dancing that had her heart suddenly stumbling. Hopefully he didn't read between the lines. Hopefully he didn't see her confusion and think that she was falling for him. No, she could not go there. She had just found a new life here that she loved, and she wasn't going to let dancing mess things up.

He grinned.

Oh goodness, that man had a beautiful grin.

"Darlin', this is a slow dance but you're fixing to spin. I'm having a great time but, between you and me, dancing is something we both love. We can come here anytime, so don't get all caught up in those deep thoughts that your brain was clearly showing me and the thundering of your heart. Even though your heart isn't pressed against me, I can feel it.

"Don't you get yourself all tied up in knots on worrying that you're making a mistake. We're having fun, you and me, and we've got a long night to go. So, hang in there, and tomorrow, after I've taken you home and dropped you off at your front door, I'm going to come out and we're going to work on a fence. But right now, as this song is ending, I'm hoping we're fixin' to do some fancy two-steppin' we'll have fun again instead of that worried look that came into those gorgeous golden eyes of yours."

And with that, he gave a little push, and twisted her to where she twirled underneath his arm. Laughing, she came back into his arms, only to be once again twisted around, and she passed one hand to another behind his back and was pulled back into his arms again.

Oh, goodness, this was a perfect night. And he was just here to have fun.

* * *

Caleb had had, as far as he was concerned, the best night of his life dancing with Jasmine tonight. He had worked hard—very hard—to keep it casual and fun when, in his heart of hearts, he wanted to pull her into his arms and slow dance the night away. She was amazing. But it was obvious that her thoughts at certain moments were clearly on keeping her distance and he had made sure he had done exactly that. This was a slow dance of life right now, and he knew it. He felt like if he had the vaguest thought—well, it wasn't vague; it was becoming a dominant thought—that he wanted this beautiful, wonderful lady in his life—well, forever more—then that meant he would take this slowly. He wouldn't dance the night away; he wouldn't dance his future away. They would take it one step at a time. And if she chose him in the end, he would be the winner in life and not the loser because he pushed too hard.

He pulled to a stop. Her porch light was on, and he glanced at her. "I'll walk you to your door." He saw the glint of a smile but also in those eyes, those telling eyes of hers, that she was worried. He wanted to say out loud, *Don't worry; I understand.*

He got out of the truck, walked around to her side, and he was glad that she hadn't tried to get out but instead let him be a gentleman. As he opened her door, he held his hand out and she slipped her hand into his. His heart thundered at simply holding her hand. Keeping her hand in his, he walked her to the door, up the two steps, and into the light. Yes, he couldn't help himself; he stepped close, placed his free arm around her shoulders, and pulled her in and gave her a soft hug. *Oh, how he hoped she didn't run from that.* Then he stepped back, still holding her hand. "I had a great night. I hope you did too."

"I did have a great night. Thank you for giving me back a night of what I've always loved." Her smile widened. "You are amazing, Caleb. And it was just great." She chuckled.

Oh, how he hoped she meant that. And in the way she said it, he really thought she did. Lifting his free hand, he cupped her cheek. "This was the best night I've had in…well, I'd tell you my life but I don't want to run you off, so I'll just say I thoroughly enjoyed it and hope you'll dance with me again. But I'm going to be here in the morning. You said you've got to get off on Saturday, and we're going to build you a fence for that little tiny donkey that you're going to take in. So you ready for that? If you have to work, I can bring my brothers—"

"No, I don't have to work. Your sweet sister-in-law can handle it tomorrow. Everybody who comes in will want a picture with her, anyway, so she told me to take off and make that sweet Daisy Duke a home, so we're going to do it."

Her smile radiated through him. "Okey dokey. I'll be here. I'll have all the stuff already on my truck—well, not my truck but my trailer. I'll hook it up and we'll get it done." And then he forced himself to step back and bring his hand back to his pocket. He reached up with his free hand that he had forced himself to let go of her and he tipped that hat of his. "Go on in now. I can't walk off the steps until I know you're into the house safely. Call me if you need me. And if not…well, I hope you don't have to need me for anything bad…"

Boy, was that a crazy thing to say. He didn't mind if she called him, if she needed him to come in and give her a hug and give her the kiss he wanted to give her so badly right now. But no; it wasn't time for that. So he stepped down on the first step as she stepped back and turned, reached into her purse, pulled out her key, unlocked that door, and stepped inside.

She looked over her shoulder. "You are an amazing man, Caleb Buckley, and I'll see you in the morning." And then she walked inside, closed the door, and waved through the window.

He turned and forced his steps to walk away. If he had it his way, this was the start of a new beginning, and he was not going to mess it up.

CHAPTER FOURTEEN

She was up at six a.m. the next morning, and fried some bacon and some eggs and wrapped them in a tortilla. They were ready when he drove up. *Goodness gracious, the man had a trailer-load of wire and post.* She hurried out the door and down the steps, laughing as he got out, grinning.

Oh, how she had had to put him out of her thoughts last night. She hadn't had such a wonderful night in…well, forever, and then he had been such a gentleman before he left, it made a mark. It made a good mark on her heart. Though she was still shaky about it, she had told herself—no, demanded—before she went to bed last night that today she would be real. She was excited, too. "Good morning. I am so really excited about this."

He climbed out of his truck, smiling. "Well, you look like you're ready to work, and that's a good thing. It's going to be easy. I'll dig the hole—I promise you, I know how. My granddaddy and my daddy all raised us to do that, so no worries. And we'll put the logs in and then we'll fill them with dirt. You'll hold the log—well, pole—while I fill the dirt in. And then, we'll roll the fence out, staple it to the wood…well, it's a staple but it takes a hammer to knock it in. Then we'll roll it to the next one and by the end of the afternoon, hopefully maybe sooner than that, we'll have Daisy Duke her own place to live. That sound good to you?"

She had clasped her hands together and grinned at him. "I can't wait. Honestly, the more I've thought about it, I'm ready, just as long as it's okay for me to have them out here on this property until I decide to either build a new place or leave."

He stopped; he had been walking to the trailer. He

spun around and looked at her with alarm on his face. "You're thinking about leaving?"

"Well, no, not really. I love it here. I don't know why that came out. Really, I don't." And she didn't, but seeing his reaction took her breath away. *He really didn't want her to leave.*

Just the idea made her smile, and then he smiled and that made her heart pump a little bit more than it was already pumping. They just stood there and looked at each other. She had to say something. "I fried some bacon and eggs and wrapped them in tortillas, if you'd like some. There's coffee and orange juice and even some grape juice, if you prefer that."

"Well, that sounds awesome. To be honest, I didn't even stop for breakfast. Normally I would go by and pick it up at the ranch but not today, so sure…I'd hate it to go to waste."

"Then follow me and we'll work extra hard because we have food in us." She spun and hurried to the house and told herself to get her head on straight. She didn't need to make that fella smile the way he had smiled because when he smiled like that, she did not want him to stop. Oh no, she did not want him to stop.

* * *

Yup, he was smiling as he strode up the steps to follow the beauty who had invited him for breakfast. She could have offered him burned eggs and bacon for all he cared; he would've eaten it and smiled the whole time.

When he walked into the cabin, he stopped. It was the first time he had been in this place in a long time. They just had leased it out to friends of the family who had wanted to come out for a while. Then, when Genna had needed a place to rent, they offered it to her because of good ole Josie Jane and Ruby and their excitement of getting this woman into town and opening her shop.

It was still a wonder to all of them that Genna had never been here but she had traveled the world as a kid with her parents and her mother and her mother's mother or her grandmother—he wasn't actually sure; he had to think back on that—had stayed here at some point when Genna's mother was a child. But Genna's mother had remembered this ranch so much and had loved the town. So when Genna had decided she was done traveling the world with her parents, she had come for a visit, and on that visit, she had met Miss Josie Jane and Ruby. They had called the ranch and set her up in a similar cabin to the one her mother had stayed in. And now Jasmine lived here.

"Wow, it's really nice in here," Caleb said. It was decorated with bright burgundy rugs and a pale-beige couch that had more pillows on it in more colors than he could even see. In that instant, he had to look at them before looking at the walls, where she had beautiful pictures hung.

He walked over to a large photo in a blue frame. "Is that a picture of Niagara Falls?"

"Actually, it is. I'm infatuated with that place. I was in high school, and I went there with my mom and dad so I could see where Dad asked Mom to marry him. There, at the base of the falls on the Canadian side. They had to put on their yellow plastic coverups or get soaked there at the base. I love the photo of the tunnels where you just go and you can see the water through the outside of the hole that you walked in. It's cool looking at the picture, but Mom said it wasn't anything like that picture right there. My mom took that picture. She enjoys taking photos. Nobody would know that since she comes and spends her time now buying antiques and shopping or setting me up to get me wherever she wants me to be." She chuckled.

"I'm glad she did that." Very glad because her sweet mother had gotten her here, and maybe one day he could thank her for the opportunity to fall for her daughter.

"Yes, me too," she paused. "So, there's a spot that you go in there under Niagara Falls, it's right on the edge as you can see in the picture, and you stand on this green grass right up next to where the falls come down. That's why in this picture you see those beautiful waves coming over the edge of Niagara Falls. And that is where Dad asked Mom to marry him. He had paid someone to come down and take his picture when he knelt and offered her the ring. It's a beautiful picture but…" She paused and her eyes looked troubled. She was a little bit nervous about something.

"And did something terrible happen?"

Her lips lifted in that sweet smile. "No. Actually, the picture is wonderful. He asked Mom to marry him and they got a great couple of pictures of him on his knee and her saying yes—they're beautiful. But, they also got this picture of the water coming over the falls by itself." She inhaled then sighed. "This sounds horrible but after my ridiculous marriage proposal fell apart, I looked at this picture in a different way. I wanted a picture of that because it represents them and their love but also for me a warning that with the wrong man instead of a happily-ever-after I messed up in trusting the wrong man. So when I came here, I hung that on my wall as a showing of all a..." She paused again.

"Well, as a reminder to me every time I walk through the front door that I'm not going to let myself fall over the ridge ever again. Mom and Dad did it right—me, I put my eye on the wrong person, and I fell from the top and ended up in the rapids down below. Well, not really, but in my heart. It reminds me of what I won't do again..."

She paused and the tears glistening in her eyes and

the words she had spoken tore at Caleb's heart. "What?" he asked, knowing she was needing to say more.

"Honestly, now I'm looking at it and I want to smile, I really do because it's like…" She waved her hand in front of her face, emotion enveloping her. And him.

He stepped forward, wrapped his arms gently around her, and tugged her close so she could lower her head to his chest and then he rested his chin on her head. "Jasmine, you can talk to me. I knew when you came here you had something deep on your mind, and I just want you to know that whatever happened, it's over. You can't live the rest of your life thinking about that dude who used you for a stupid dance competition. He took feelings that you had for him, and he obviously went crazy with it and got you believing he felt the same way about you." He wished he could meet up with the worthless dude.

He leaned back and lifted her chin so she was looking in his eyes. "He should probably become an award-winning actor because, Jasmine, dear lady, you are *not* stupid. So whatever that dude did, it was good—

it convinced you that he loved you. And as much as I don't want to say it, he had to be good. But I can promise you, I hope that when the right man comes along and you feel something for him in that beautiful, wonderful heart that's inside your chest, that you will not let that creep take your joy and that other fella's joy away. Now, come on, what did you realize about that picture just now? I have to know."

"I look at it now, and I see hope. I see, just like last night dancing with a happy cowboy, I saw happiness last night in something I used to love and lost. And now, looking at that picture, I see hope and I see what I hope is my future."

His heart was going berserk. It wasn't like he was going over the falls; he was on the rapids, going fast and furious down those rapids. He smiled because, in his heart, he knew when he got to the end of those rapids, he was going to catch her before she made it to the bottom.

They stared at each other, their hearts pounding against each other's, and time stood still.

* * *

Oh, the man had a way with words. Her heart pounded erratically, drumming away and telling her to dive in, to climb over that edge of that waterfall and just dive. *This time,* she knew she wouldn't hit bottom.

This time, those beautiful, thick waves of mist would interrupt and carry her into the arms she really longed to be in. "Caleb, I think I love you."

His heart thundered against hers and she hoped that she hadn't made the wrong move. But as bad as her record was, knowing that, yes, she had been stupid once, right now she didn't think so. And as she watched his smile spread, lifting up into that wide, crooked grin of his, beneath that rugged cowboy hat, her heart started to dance because she knew—she hadn't been wrong.

"Darlin', I love you. I think I've loved you from the moment we met, and I just didn't know it because you were ignoring me. But it drew me, just wondering what would make such a sweet, beautiful person who loved to chat and talk with everybody but a guy…I had to figure out why. I knew someone hurt you." He cupped her face between his hands. "I love you. I'll say it again, and I'll say it for the rest of your life. We're going to build your temporary donkey fence then later we'll build a huge area at *our* place. But, right now, if you'll let me, I want to kiss you. So when you say I can I will but only then."

Oh, how she loved this man! He hadn't rushed her; he hadn't coerced her, and he wasn't even going to kiss her until she said he was the right one. She wrapped her hand around his neck and looked deep into those . "Please, kiss me."

And with that, he lowered his lips to hers, his fingers cupping her cheek as he kissed her gently. She felt his heart thundering against hers and thank goodness she knew he was just being gentle because of her being soft—but she wanted more! Her heart exploded as she slid her arms around his waist, and she returned his kiss with all the enthusiasm he had put in her heart. Because she knew this time, without a doubt, she wasn't wrong.

He deepened the kiss with his reply, and she felt him smile against her lips. She chuckled and broke contact as she looked into his eyes. "Oh, Caleb, thank you. Not only am I getting to do this with a wonderful man I love, but you're making me so very grateful that that crazy man didn't marry me. I was so out of it, so lost in my thoughts…I could have messed up my whole entire life."

His grin widened. "Jasmine, I'm going to tell you something I believe with all my heart. If you *had* married that dude, you'd have figured out that he'd been using you and I'm fairly certain you'd be single right now no matter what. That's a hard thing to say—some people don't look at divorce as a good thing but sometimes it can't be helped. And what I'm saying is that because now I know you love me, I hope you don't think I'm stupid like that dude was and kick me to the curb." He hitched his brow.

She couldn't help it; she laughed so hard she had to back up, bend over, and put her elbows on her knees to stay standing. He was laughing too as she finally rose up and smiled at this crazy cowboy. "All I can say is you tell it like it is and I'm ready for that. So now what?"

In that moment, he went down on his knee, holding

her hand, and looked up at her. "Jasmine, will you do me the honor and make me the happiest man in the world? Say you'll marry me. I'll get you as many donkeys and goats as you want. We'll make that little donkey happy as long as I can make you happy."

Heart pounding, hands trembling she squeezed his hand. "I don't think I could ever be any happier than I am right now. Yes! I had no idea coming here was going to make me have the happy ending I had hoped to have. I love you, and I cannot wait to become your wife."

EPILOGUE

Jasmine was getting married to the cowboy, the man…oh what a man he was of her dreams.

As she stood there inside Josie Jane's Wash & Repeat where everyone gathered when Josie Jane sent word out to come on over. She looked around at everyone who had been rooting for her. There was Ruby, sweet Ruby and Josie Jane then there was long, tall Millie, cowgirl extraordinaire. There was Genna, Sydney, and Kelsy, all of who would soon be her sisters-in-laws. Her family. Then sitting in the chair beside Kelsy was Arabella, the person she needed to talk to.

Around the room were all the other sweet women she'd come to love. They were older and came to all the dances and sat in their lawn chairs near the drink and snack tables, knitting, crocheting or just talking and watching everything going on around them. They had so much fun watching everyone on dance night and they also loved coming into the store and letting her help them pick out beautiful outfits. But as she turned and smiled at all of them she let her gaze rest on sweet Arabella.

The tiny woman owned the bakery in town. She was a wonderful baker and Jasmine wanted to ask her if she would bake her wedding cake. "Arabella," she said, walking over and smiling down at the sweet lady.

Kelsy's watched from her chair beside the wonderful baker. "I bet I can guess what you're going to ask Ms. Arabella," she said as if reading Jasmine's mind. Her grin made Jasmine's smile widen.

"Yes, I'm sure you can. Ms. Arabella, I want to ask if you would make my wedding cake? Your cakes are amazing and it would make my wonderful dream day even more special."

Arabella got a sad look in her eyes, she reached out and took Jasmine's hand between her two hands. She gently patted the top of Jasmine's hand with the hand she had on top and with the hand beneath Jasmine's she squeezed tightly. Jasmine suddenly had a bad feeling. What was going on?

Her gaze went to Kelsy, who she knew could see what was happening since their hands were right in front of her eyes. Kelsy looked stunned too as she studied Ms. Arabella.

"My dear, sweet girl. You know I have loved to bake all of my life. And you also know that I've been trying to hold out on finding someone to come in and buy my bakery and carry on what I've loved so much. But, that person hasn't shown up. And therefore, I decided last night…and though I'm not real happy with myself for telling you this…I'm not going to bake anymore."

"What?" she gasped and many others in the room did too. Jasmine's gazed locked with Josie Jane's and she saw that Josie wasn't surprised. Her gaze moved to Ruby who also wasn't surprised. "Are you alright?"

"My legs get tired," Arabella continued, gently drawing her gaze back. "And though my heart is with you and your joy right now, my heart isn't in the baking any longer. I want to sit here with my friends chatting and knitting and enjoying my life sitting instead of standing and baking my life away. So please, please, sweet dear, don't be angry with me. I know that there are a lot of other wonderful bakeries in the surrounding towns. Just none other in this town, which is such a shame. But you and your future sisters-in-laws can all drive over and have fun picking it out and then one of them, I'm sure, will be happy to go get it or maybe one of the places would deliver it. I'm confident it will be wonderful. So please don't take this as something it's not, I love you, dear, and have so enjoyed your company there in our sidelined dance watching. But I'm thrilled you're going to marry the Happy Dancin' Cowboy of yours. Y'all are going to dance your hearts away and I'm going to sit there with all these other buddies of mine and watch. I'm just not going to bake your cake."

Her heart was clenching, she was in so much disbelief. Yes, she'd known the sweet lady was looking for someone to buy her place, and the hunt had gone on for a little while now. But no one had come to town looking to buy the bakery. Now, she sighed. Now, oh goodness, she was going to retire and Jasmine was so happy for her. Yes, she could find a cake somewhere else it just wouldn't be her wonderful creation.

It wouldn't be Arabella's cake.

She pushed that aside and knelt down. While everyone watched and remained silent she took control of the still clutched hands, placing her free hand on top of the wonderful Arabella's. "I love you dearly, you sweet lady. And though I know I'll never find a cake as good as yours or a heart like yours, I totally understand. Sometimes, when it's time to change your life its time. And I'm happy for you. You are going to enjoy all of your free time, and I know that one day someone out there is going to come along and buy your wonderful bakery. Goodness, if I could bake, which I can't, I would buy it and go into business. But right now I'm happy for you, so don't you feel bad about not baking my cake. Me and Kelsy right here and Genna and Sydney will take a girls' day out and test cakes until we find the exact one. Right, Kelsy?" She grinned at Kelsy knowing she'd join in.

But, her friend had a stunned look on her face and as they stared at each other, Kelsy's eyes brightened and her smile widened. "No, Jasmine. I know exactly who can bake your cake. Arabella, if I get my sweet friend Violet to come here, can she bake it in that amazing bakery of yours? I've been wanting Violet to come here since the day I moved here. She's wonderful and has a sweet daddy who is one of the best bakers in all of Texas but is now in a wheelchair. She supports the both of them and works for a horrible man who takes advantage of their situation. In my heart, I know she would be perfect for our wonderful town and I've been trying to convince her. But she's hesitant. So," she said, looking around at everyone with her eyes twinkling.

"What?" Ruby asked, with a big grin.

"Well, here's the deal, I'm going to invite her to come bake this wedding cake. I know she'll come because she knows it means a lot to me. She'll come fill in for sweet Arabella in baking our future sister-in-law's cake and I hope that just maybe after she's done that she will make the right decision about her life. And that will be to change her life and move here. So what do y'all say, think that's a good idea?"

Jasmine could feel Arabella squeeze her hand and

they grinned at each other. "I am completely in. Because as y'all know I understand what moving to this fantastic town can do for someone. It helped me make it through so much and many of y'all did too. So if your friend needs to do that too, then that is what we are going to do. You invite her. Are you in?"

Arabella was all smiles. "I am *in* and I'm so excited. Kelsy, you get your friend here and my clean, spotless bakery is hers to work in and hopefully—and I'm pretty sure I'm right on this, we'll have a bunch of wonderful people urging her on while she's baking your cake, Jasmine. And maybe, just maybe she'll realize that she wants to live here and I'll make her a great deal on my little bakery. Because just from the look in your eyes, Kelsy, I have a feeling she will be perfect. And that's what I want. For whoever carries on my wonderful shop to love it and this town as much as I do. So let's do this."

Not only do we get to have an exciting wedding, we're going to get to meet someone new and help them fall in love with our town, my bakery, and who knows…maybe one of our sweet cowboys."

Everyone was laughing and smiling. Millie stepped

up, the big tall woman stuffed both hands on her blue jean-clad hips and grinned down at them. "I think this is a brilliant, perfect idea. We all know that here in Lone Star, Texas, dreams are made. And I have to tell y'all that my heart is kind of feelin' that a dream is workin' hard inside of it. So, let's do this. And who knows whose life, besides sweet Jasmine's, is also going to change. So come on, ladies, let's get ready to host a wedding and meet and see our new baker. Because I'm going to think positive, I have a feeling that she cannot do anything but fall in love with this town."

Jasmine hugged a smiling Arabella, then she stood, grinned at Millie as the tall cowgirl enveloped her in a hug and everyone around them watched. She leaned back smiling into this wonderful woman's eyes, the woman who had lost the love of her life to an angry bull, hidden in her shop, and then when the dances began, she'd helped plan them all.

She talked to many of the new brides at their wedding, talked many words of encouragement, and then helped sweet Kelsy fall in love with Ace... And maybe what she was saying now was that she and

Kelsy's grandfather, Lumas, might really be thinking of taking the next step. While they all brought Kelsy's friend here to bake her and Caleb's wedding cake.

"You are a true inspiration you, tall cowgirl, you. You helped me through so much and I just see even more great things coming. Thank you. I love you dearly."

She looked about the room taking in everyone. "I love you all. I'm glad to be here and I cannot wait to become Mrs. Caleb Buckley, the Happy Dancin' Cowboy's wife."

Everyone laughed and she was embraced by them all one at a time… Life was a dream come true, and she was ready to dance happily-ever-after with the man of her dreams.

More Books by Hope Moore

Billionaire Cowboys of Lone Star, Texas

Forever Love'n Cowboy

Sweet Love'n Cowboy

Heart Love'n Cowboy

Love Catch'n Cowboy

McCoy Billionaire Brothers

Her Billionaire Cowboy's Fake Marriage

Her Billionaire Cowboy's Fake Wedding Fiasco

Her Billionaire Cowboy's Trouble in Paradise

Her Billionaire Cowboy's Secret Baby Surprise

Her Billionaire Cowboy's Second Chance Romance

Her Billionaire Cowboy Fake Fiancé

Her Billionaire Cowboy's Inconvenient Marriage Blessing

Billionaire Cowboys of True Love, Texas

Billionaire Cowboy's Runaway Bride

Billionaire Cowboy's Wedding Crasher

Her Billionaire Cowboy's Hill Country Proposal

Billionaire Cowboy Auctioned at Christmas

Billionaire Cowboy's Dream Come True

Happy Dance'n Cowboy (Book 4)

Real Love'n Cowboy (Book 5)

About the Author

Hope Moore is the pen name of an award-winning author who lives deep in the heart of Texas surrounded by Christian cowboys who give her inspiration for all of her inspirational sweet romances. She loves writing clean & wholesome, swoon worthy romances for all of her fans to enjoy and share with everyone. Her heartwarming, feel good romances are full of humor and heart, and gorgeous cowboys and heroes to love. And the spunky women they fall in love with and live happily-ever-after.

When she isn't writing, she's trying very hard not to cook, since she could live on peanut butter sandwiches, shredded wheat, coffee...and cheesecake why should she cook? She loves writing though and creating new stories is her passion. Though she does love shoes, she's admitted she has an addiction and tries really hard to stay out of shoe stores. She, however, is not addicted to social media and chooses to write instead of surf FB - but she LOVES her readers so she's working on a free novella just for you and if you sign up for her newsletter she will send it to you as soon as its ready! You'll also receive snippets of her adventures, along with special deals, sneak peaks of soon-to-be released books and of course any sales she might be having.

She promises she will not spam you, she hates to be spammed also, so she wouldn't dare do that to people she's crazy about (that means YOU). You can unsubscribe at any time.

Sign up for my newsletter here!

I can't wait to hear from you.

Hope Moore~
Always hoping for more love, laughter and reading for you every day of your life!

www.ingramcontent.com/pod-product-compliance
Lightning Source LLC
Chambersburg PA
CBHW070647100726
47907CB00007B/2129